VOICE
LESSONS

A Memoir in Essays

MIROLAND IMPRINT 47

ONTARIO ARTS COUNCIL
CONSEIL DES ARTS DE L'ONTARIO

an Ontario government agency
un organisme du gouvernement de l'Ontario

Canada Council   Conseil des arts
for the Arts   du Canada

Guernica Editions Inc. acknowledges the support of
the Canada Council for the Arts and the Ontario Arts Council.
The Ontario Arts Council is an agency of the Government of Ontario.

We acknowledge the financial support of the Government of Canada.

EVE KRAKOW

VOICE LESSONS

A Memoir in Essays

MiroLand
p.u.b.l.i.s.h.e.r.s

TORONTO • CHICAGO
BUFFALO • LANCASTER (U.K.)
2024

*Author Note: Although this is a work of creative nonfiction,
some of the names and details have been changed
to protect people's privacy.*

Guernica Founder: Antonio D'Alfonso

Michael Mirolla, general editor
Kulamrit Bamrah, editor
Cover design and interior design: Rafael Chimicatti

Guernica Editions Inc.
1241 Marble Rock Rd., Gananoque, ON K7G 2V4
2250 Military Road, Tonawanda, N.Y. 14150-6000 U.S.A.
www.guernicaeditions.com

Distributors:
Independent Publishers Group (IPG)
600 North Pulaski Road, Chicago IL 60624
University of Toronto Press Distribution (UTP)
5201 Dufferin Street, Toronto (ON), Canada M3H 5T8

First edition.
Printed in Canada.

Legal Deposit—Third Quarter
Library of Congress Catalog Card Number: 2024931054
Library and Archives Canada Cataloguing in Publication
Title: Voice lessons : a memoir in essays / Eve Krakow.
Names: Krakow, Eve, author.
Description: "MiroLand imprint, 47."
Identifiers: Canadiana (print) 20240297989 | Canadiana (ebook) 20240298047
ISBN 9781771838924 (softcover) | ISBN 9781771838931 (EPUB)
Subjects: LCSH: Krakow, Eve. | CSH: Authors, Canadian (English)
—21st century—Biography. | LCGFT: Autobiographies.
Classification: LCC PS8621.R35 Z46 2024 | DDC C814/.6—dc23

Contents

PART I
IN SEARCH OF A VOICE

How to Summarize Your Life in Three Metro Stops

YOU'RE SITTING IN A WINDOW seat of the metro car, elbow against the murky black window and head resting in your hand. You're half-asleep, warmly nestled in your winter ski jacket and scarf, knapsack on your knees, mundane details of the day's work ahead and thoughts of bittersweet coffee drifting through your mind's haze.

The metro doors jerk open and out of instinct you look up, a brief glance, expecting to see the usual ebb and flow of bleary-eyed commuters.

And there he is, unmistakable, even though it's been maybe ten years since you last bumped into each other: his tall, thin frame, slightly tilted head, well-groomed blond hair and arresting blue eyes. He is the picture of the young, successful professional in his dark suit and overcoat, black briefcase in hand and confident stride.

Your heart beats faster, your senses now alert.

He sees you and his face breaks into a smile.

He sits down beside you. For several seconds you look at each other, grinning. Where to begin?

"So, what are you up to?" he says finally.

His voice is much deeper than you remember, and it throws you off. How does one summarize one's life, who they are, what they've become? "I, uh, well …"

In that fraction of a second you detect a shimmer of condescension in the corner of his eye, an arrogant awareness of his personal success. As if he's waiting to see if you have grown beyond the awkward, blundering self you were in high school.

You must say something to prove yourself. You want to tell him about your singing lessons, about the joy and intensity at last Sunday's master class, about your plans to travel, about your dreams of saving the world ... But you sense the question is really about work and so, finally, you say, "I'm self-employed. Translation and editing."

"Really?! That's funny, because—"

You suspect that whatever he's about to say is irrelevant, because translation is what you do but it is not who you are. At best it's only a small part of who you are.

"—I'm an associate at a small advertising company in Old Montreal. Well, not exactly small. By now we have twenty-four people. Do you ever do advertising copy?"

You do sometimes but it's not what you prefer. You tell him as much.

"More corporate stuff, then?"

Yes, you say, and also some work for the Ministry of Education. "A newsletter sent out to schools and teachers." But it's so much more than that, and you think of the team of freelancers you work with, the long nights crammed into a hotel room after conferences, the feverish writing of articles for publication the next day, the elation of being part of something—

"Do you have any kids?" he asks.

You shake your head and laugh.

He has two, he tells, a boy and a girl.

Of course, you think. You are the fallen woman, divorced and childless at age thirty-one. It's not that you don't want a family.

You ask how old his kids are.

"My boy is six and my little girl just turned two." He smiles as he says this, picturing them in his mind. It's clear that he is happy.

"Yes, things are going very well," he says, to himself as much as to you.

Suddenly, you feel the bulkiness of your coat, the weight of your tattered knapsack, the unkempt tangle of your hair. You are mesmerized by how deep his voice has become, the boy turned man.

He asks if you've been in touch with anyone from high school and you launch into a roundabout story. Then the metro stops at a station.

"Oh! This is my stop," you say, caught off-guard.

For a moment, time slows. Hovers.

Should you stay and continue the conversation? You've already said this is your stop. The metro doors wait open.

Shrugging and apologizing and laughing, you dash off.

"See you 'round," you both say. And then you're on the platform and the doors have shut. You've told him nothing of who you really are.

Your ears fill with the deafening rush of the train gathering speed and heading into the tunnel. Then you stand alone in the station's echoey silence.

But it's easy for him, you think. His life fits into neat little sentences. Fits the mould down to the very brand of cologne (or so you imagine, you didn't actually notice). While for you, there seems to be no mould. You scorn him for it and yet what is the harm if he is happy?

Besides, who is to judge, based on a few sentences between metro stops?

The Understudy

AMY STANDS CENTRE STAGE in jeans and a black t-shirt, listening to the director's instructions.

As I watch from the sidelines, my fingers cling to the smooth pages of the script. I try to ignore the longing curled up inside, a ball so tight that my stomach aches. A creature that wants to break free, to unfurl itself, to soar, but is terrified to do so.

I edge closer, careful not to drop the pages in my grip.

I'm at a rehearsal for the Gilbert and Sullivan operetta *Iolanthe*. The community theatre group meets in the church hall once a week. The room is a mix of old and new, with its lemon-scented tiled floor, dark wood trim, and heavy, musty curtains framing high windows.

I'm clumped off to one side with the rest of the chorus, waiting for our turn to sing. But while the other women fidget, whisper, and giggle, my attention is on Amy. She plays Leila, one of the principal fairies.

In the actual show, the women—the fairies—will be dressed in wispy dresses and gauzy shawls, while the men—peers in the House of Lords—will wear robes and powdered wigs. At the moment though, most of the cast are lounging about in jeans and sweaters.

I am Amy's understudy. This means that although I sing in the chorus, I must also learn the part of Leila and be ready to step in at any time.

Amy nods to something the director has said. Satisfied, the director turns back to the group and claps his hands twice. "Okay, everyone, from the top of the scene."

The piano starts. I join the chorus singing, "*Tripping hither, tripping thither,*" moving left and moving right with the group, trying not to trip on my own feet. But when we pause our dance for Amy/Leila's solo, my body stiffens.

"*If you ask us how we live, lovers all essentials give,*" Amy says, as she steps forward from the fairy circle.

My eyes follow Amy's body as she glides from one part of the stage to another, in time to the song's metre. "*We can ride on lovers' sighs, warm ourselves in lovers' eyes …*"

From my place in the background, I speak the words just loud enough for my own ears. I subtly mirror the gestures, imitating the movements in a faint echo, trying to etch them into my being.

I've wanted to sing in a musical ever since I was a child. My parents used to bring me to local amateur productions. I'd perch on the edge of my chair, captivated by the music, absorbed in the emotion of the singer exposing their deepest longings, desires, and inner conflicts. At every show, something inside me would stir, sit up and latch on to that moment, never wanting to let go.

I wanted to be that singer. I wanted to be that person onstage.

When I was a bit older and would find myself at home alone, I'd belt out Broadway songs as loud as I could, twirling and leaping about the house. Then, I'd bow to the curtain calls of my imaginary audience.

In real life though, I am not that person. I am quiet and shy. I blush when someone speaks to me. I hover in the background and stumble over my feet.

But that's precisely it: When I sing, I am free. In that release of air and sound, my whole body thrums. It starts in my chest and moves outward, a current racing through my arms to my fingertips, flowing down my legs and rooting me to the ground. The resonance clears my mind, and through those words and notes, all the tightness balled up inside me surges out. All those feelings trapped inside come rushing out, released from their confines, expanding, soaring. I find expression and fulfilment in a way not possible with words alone.

A sharp pain jolts me back to the present—an elbow jabbing into my upper arm.

"Sorry about that," Helen says. "We have to turn here, remember? I go here, and you go over there."

Helen has short dark hair and wears a striped turtleneck sweater. She's a bit of a mother-figure to the group, always checking in on the younger and older actors alike as if we were her children.

"Oh, right," I say, my face growing hot. "Sorry."

Helen smiles. "Don't worry, you'll get the hang of it."

The song is over and we've moved on to the dialogue. Amy takes centre stage again with two other fairies and the Fairy Queen. She speaks in a loud, clear voice. She laughs when she fumbles her lines and jokes with the director. Then she pushes her straight blond hair back behind her ears and tries again, this time getting it right.

How I envy that hair. My own is dark and frizzy and never behaves.

In truth, I recognize why Amy got the part. Although she's a few years younger than me, she has a lot more theatre experience. I've sung in choirs and shows before, and even had a few solos, but I'm not an actress. When I'm in a scene, I suddenly feel the empty air on my skin. I become all too aware of my body alone in that space and don't know what to do. My limbs turn to rubber and I forget my lines.

Kind of like in real life.

Still, I can't help feeling resentful, even jealous. It's a silly show, really, but ...

At break, I sit on the floor, back to the wall and binder propped up against my knees, reviewing my notes. I bite into an apple and steal glances at Amy over the top of my pages. She's standing in the middle of the room, laughing with another cast member. Amy chats with everyone. In her everyday life she's a Grade 1 teacher. I can just picture her ample form presiding over a classroom of noisy children, showing them how to trace their letters, intervening in fights over crayons, getting little Jimmy to go wipe his runny nose.

Meanwhile, at thirty-two, I feel like I'm still trying to get my career off the ground. I originally studied journalism but somehow veered off course and ended up as an office assistant. For the past two years I've been pitching stories to newspapers and magazines, and while I've written a few articles, none have led to steady work. It's like I'm still trying to figure out "what I want to be when I grow up." Still trying to get my personal life off the ground, too, hoping to find that special someone.

I'm pretty sure Amy has a boyfriend.

At the next rehearsal, Amy arrives as usual, announcing her presence with a big "Hi everyone!" as she throws her coat over a chair.

My eyes track her movements. All week, I've been trying to practise the "tripping hither" solo at home and fretting over the timing of the steps and gestures. Now, heart beating fast—which makes me sound out of breath—I tap Amy on the shoulder and ask if we can go over it together.

It's not that Amy isn't nice to me, but we usually don't talk much or hang out with the same people. Sometimes I feel she is merely tolerating my presence.

So I'm relieved when she says that she'd be happy to review the steps with me.

I'm expecting to do so discreetly in a corner, but Amy strides to an open space in the middle of the room. "Shall we try it from the top?"

I nod.

Once we start, my body begins to relax. I copy Amy's movements, listen to her tips and take copious notes. She's a good teacher, encouraging me along—though I get the feeling that she's treating me like one of her elementary school students.

It occurs to me that some leads might feel reluctant to share their secrets with their understudy, but clearly, I am no threat. I'm not sure whether to feel indignant or grateful. For now, I am merely resigned.

At the end of rehearsal, I can't find my binder. My precious binder with my music and lines and stage directions and detailed notes and ...

I turn my head this way and that, frantic. People are leaving with binders under their arms. *Maybe someone took mine by mistake.* Panic starts to rise in my throat. Amy, putting on her jacket, sees my distress.

"What's wrong?" she asks, releasing a sigh of exasperation.

My face reddens. "My binder. I can't find it." I'm embarrassed to be blinking back tears.

Amy climbs onto a chair and shouts in her clear teacher voice, "Has anyone seen Eve's binder? Please check that you don't have it."

People pause in their shuffling. They flip open their binders to check, shake their heads, lift jackets from chairs, peer into their bags. Nothing.

"Thanks," I say, as she's getting down from the chair.

Amy shrugs. "I'm sure it'll turn up."

After everyone has left, I find it. It's perched on the window ledge, hiding behind the piano. I must have left it on a chair and then someone moved it. It sits there like a lost, scared puppy. I pick it up gently and tuck it into my knapsack.

I do not stop to wonder what it is that I'm really trying to keep safe and sound.

Being an understudy is tricky because I don't get many chances to rehearse the part onstage with the other actors or accompanying musicians. I watch and observe and try to learn. Then I practise on my own, without context.

I scrutinize Amy's tone and gestures. Onstage and off.

It's something I find myself doing more and more: watching others, observing. Trying to understand the social cues, the expectations, how people talk to each other and respond. Trying to learn a script I was never given.

Two weeks from showtime, it happens. Amy comes down with the flu.

Rehearsal begins, and when we get to the scenes with Leila, I step forward. My heart hammers in my chest and my knees threaten to give way. But I open my mouth, deliver my lines, and sing the part. I perform the movements, hands trembling, legs shaking. My voice wobbles and my face is on fire, but I make it through.

After the run-through, the director pauses to talk to me. "Good job," he says. "Keep at it."

That creature inside me perks up its ears, uncurling just a little.

In the end, Amy makes a swift recovery and is back at rehearsal the following week.

The tightness in my shoulders dissolves and my lungs fill with relief.

It's opening night, almost time to take our places. I'm looking for the seamstress to help me adjust my fairy wings, which keep sliding down. I glance into the dressing room reserved for the female leads. Fumes of hairspray hang in the air.

And that's when I see her.

Amy is staring at herself in the mirror, murmuring her lines. But it is the tremor in her voice that makes me pause. I steal a glance at her reflection. A vein pulses at her temple. Her hands are trembling.

Realization hits me with a jolt. She's nervous.

I move away quickly before she sees me. But as I continue down the hall, pulling at the shoulder strap of my costume, the aftershock ripples through me.

Confident, popular, self-assured Amy is nervous.

It will not be the only time I meet with such a revelation. The following season, I will be shocked to come across our male lead pacing and fretting. "You'll be fine," Helen will reassure him, hands adjusting his wig, as he looks to her with pleading eyes.

Years later, just before a choir concert, I will stumble upon the soloist warming up his voice in the stairwell. He will be shaking out his hands and taking deep breaths, trying to calm himself down. Again, my brain will struggle to match the image of the confident, joking baritone of rehearsals with the man in front of me, anxious and vulnerable.

In fact, I will need to see such evidence time and time again before the creature inside me dares to truly break free.

It will be the same story when I have children and see other mothers dressed in sharp outfits, not a hair out of place, who always seem to know exactly what to do and what to say.

It will be some time before I finally realize how universal my deepest insecurities really are.

But all of that is in the future.

For now, the seed has been planted. I carry it with me as I take my place backstage with the chorus, unsure of what to do with it or what it means. It is a crack, a hairline fracture in my wall of beliefs. Because if someone is nervous about performing a part that they have rehearsed and practised and taken hours to refine, then what else ...?

My heart is pounding. I can smell the burning spotlights. I wipe my damp palms on my costume.

But the music has already started.

It's time to step out onto the stage.

Songs of My Childhood

SIDE A
Track #1 ▪ Mary Had a Little Lamb

Nursery school.

I'm standing in the middle of a huge room. My nostrils fill with smells of plasticine and glue. There are children everywhere. Children building towers with blocks. Children in smocks finger-painting at easels. Toy trucks go vroom.

On a raised platform, a girl has her arms elbow-deep in a large bin of sudsy water. She and a boy are playing with white and blue plastic containers, pouring water from one to another. Foamy bubbles cling to their skin.

I love bubbles. I want to play in those bubbles. But my feet are rooted to the spot.

SIDE B
Track #1 ▪ Old MacDonald Had a Farm

When did the music begin? Did my mother sing to me? My sisters? During family car rides to the country house, on summer road trips, there were always songs …

Track #2 ▪ I Am a Candle (that lights the others)

Kindergarten.

A paper crown with a cardboard candle encircles my head. I coloured it myself.

We're putting on a show for our parents for Chanukah. I'm standing on a chair, looking out at the row of parents, some still in their coats, purses on their laps, sitting on chairs that are too small for them.

I don't know how to go over there, how to approach the girl, or the teacher. I can't move. I can't, I can't! I don't know what to do, everyone is busy, busy, busy, where is mommy, I want mommy! My insides hurt, my face hurts.

Hot tears are sliding down my cheeks before I can stop them.

Track #2 ▪ One, Two, Buckle My Shoe

Grade 1.

It's after lunch and we're supposed to be playing. Everyone else is at the back of the classroom, pushing trucks across the carpet, stacking blocks, dressing up dolls. I sit at my desk waiting for the teacher to give us work. This is school. I want to work.

"Why don't you go play with the other children?" the teacher tries. I shake my head. Then I feel the tears coming and put my head down on my desk, tucking it under my arms. The hard surface is cool against my skin. It smells of eraser and the apple I had for a snack.

My insides are swirling with excitement. Four classmates stand on either side of me: together we form a menorah. I'm standing on a chair, higher than everyone else.

I sing a song explaining that I'm the *shamash*, the candle used to light the others. I stick out my chest, pointing to it as I sing. My first solo. In that moment, I'm thrilled to be the centre of attention.

Looking back, I wonder what was going through my teachers' minds. The child who never speaks.

Track #3 ▪ Getting to Know You

Growing up, every year at the country house, I go with my family to see musical productions put on by the local theatre group: *Annie Get Your Gun*, *Brigadoon*, *Oklahoma!* The plots and jokes go over my head, but I am captivated by the musical numbers.

I sit on the edge of my wooden chair, drinking in the songs of these men and women as they lay bare their hearts, share their anguish, celebrate their triumphs.

It isn't just that I don't feel like playing with the other children. I don't know how.

Why can't we do more math? I love math. The numbers fall neatly into place.

Out of the corner of my eye, I see Trudy approaching, pigtails bobbing. We were in pre-kindergarten together. I burrow my face further into my arms. I hear her body brush the side of my desk as she leans in. She peers at me curiously. "What's wrong?"

I can smell the fruit punch on her breath. I don't answer. Peeking through the tiny space under my arm, I watch her walk away, back to the others.

Track #3 ▪ Rock Around the Clock

In Grade 2, Miss Conway teaches us how to play the ukulele. I hug the instrument close to my body. It's small enough for my seven-year-old fingers to reach around the neck.

It's different from a guitar. You strum with your index finger. Miss Conway teaches us to play "Ezekiel Saw the Wheel,"

I am mesmerized by the way the chorus sings and dances, together as one, words and movements falling neatly into place.

I want to be up there with them.

I sit rapt, trying to absorb every note.

Year after year, we go to shows put on by my aunt's troupe in the city: *Oliver*, *Annie*, *The King and I*.

After dinner at my aunt's house, my sisters and I gather around her piano and she teaches us the harmonies. She teaches us "Getting to Know You." When we get to "*You are precisely ...*" she pauses, lifting her hand from the keys and tracing an arc high in the air to guide me in the solo phrase, "*... my cup of tea.*"

Track #4 ▪ The Sun'll Come Out Tomorrow

After my mother dies, I often arrive home from school before my older sisters. The house is empty. I fill the space with music.

"My Grandma's Feather Bed,"
and "Rock Around the Clock."
The skin below my fingernail
becomes chafed and raw but I
don't care.

The following year she starts a
choir. We rehearse at lunchtime,
singing the songs in unison. Miss
Conway leads and we follow.

In December, we sing Christmas
carols for our parents. We perform at a school board event.

One day we get to miss classes to
perform at Plaza Bonaventure,
downtown. As we file onto the
stage, my whole body quivers, the
thrill of being part of something
special almost too much to bear.

Track #4 ▪ Billie Jean

High school.

As I walk past the lockers of the
popular kids, I hear them talking
about a party they were at on
the weekend. How do all the
popular kids end up with their
lockers together? The lockers
are assigned by last name, alpha-
betical order. Mine is down the
hall and around the corner.

I belt out Broadway songs at
the top of my lungs: "The Sun'll
Come Out Tomorrow" (*Annie*),
"I'd Do Anything" (*Oliver*),
"Wouldn't It Be Loverly" (*My
Fair Lady*), "Wonder of Wonders"
(*Fiddler on the Roof*), "Doe, A
Deer" (*The Sound of Music*),
"I Sing the Body Electric" (*Fame*).

I act out the parts and dance
around our open living-dining
room to my own choreography.

I bow to standing ovations.

I pull out what is deep inside and
launch it out into the world.

Track #5 ▪ Rock Around the Clock (reprise)

I'm standing in the hallway at
my high school, staring at a
cartoon drawing of a turntable,
notes drifting up and away. It's
an invitation to audition for a
'50s show. To sing, dance or do
a comedy skit.

My stomach begins to churn
with excitement.

I bring my ukulele to the audition and perform a song that
my Grade 2 teacher taught me:

I wasn't invited to the party, of course. I never am.

Vanessa is waiting. She's an outlier like me, but not because she's awkward and shy. She's just ... eccentric. She wears flowing shawls and billowing silk outfits and she is not afraid to speak her mind. She wants to be a professional violinist and practises several hours a day. The other kids respect her for that.

"Guess what!" she says. "I have the new single, 'Billie Jean'!"

Vanessa is obsessed with Michael Jackson. She tries to imitate his dance moves but the result is just embarrassing.

That night, we listen to the record in her basement, a tiny room draped in burgundy and velvet. We hug sequined cushions to our chests and talk about the boys we have crushes on. We dwell for hours on a single sentence they uttered, or a look exchanged, picking it apart, searching for a message that isn't there.

"Rock Around the Clock."
The organizers, older students in Grades 10 and 11, are thrilled.

Over the next few weeks, during lunch hour and after school, I slip through the doors of the auditorium. Only people in the show are allowed to watch the rehearsals.

When the bell rings I stumble past the lockers of the popular kids. My face turns hot as I feel their eyes on my awkward clothes and hair.

I hurry to class and bury my face in my books, scribbling answers to problems in physics and math. I engross myself in the predictable logic of numbers.

The show's directors decide to create a choreography of three couples swing dancing behind me. While I sing and strum and get used to the microphone, they practise their steps on the dusty black stage.

I become friends with Gordon. He's in Grade 10. He walks over after the first rehearsal, fringes of his dark hair damp, and skin shining with perspiration.

Track #5 ▪ A Day in the Life

I'm at Nathalie's house, along with her best friend Claire. I met them at a theatre festival for teens—we're in a show together.

Claire is a talented actress but offstage she strikes me as prim and reserved. Her blond hair is tied back in a ponytail, her blouse buttoned and tucked in. Nathalie is her antithesis, as outgoing as her long red hair, loose and wild. She wears flouncy hippy skirts, Indian cotton blouses and bead necklaces.

I am not a very good actress. My body feels like soggy cheese and the director glares at my incompetence. But in this show, I get to sing in a quartet. My saving grace.

We sit on the hardwood floor of Nathalie's second-floor bedroom, a breeze from the open window caressing our heads. Nathalie digs out a Beatles record, slides it from the cardboard sleeve and places it on a turntable. "This is our favourite song," she tells me, adjusting the needle.

"Where'd you learn to play?" he asks, chin nodding at my ukulele. I tell him about my Grade 2 teacher, Miss Conway. He's impressed that I've kept it up all these years. "You have a great voice," he tells me. My face flushes hot as I mumble a thanks.

Gordon is friendly and chatty. I don't have to search for things to say. He tells me that he's never danced much before, but the girls needed partners, so he volunteered. It's hard work but he's having a blast.

The night of the show, I don the flared skirt and polka-dot blouse the senior students have picked out for me. A Grade 11 girl does my make-up. I wait in the wings amid props and wires, breathing in hairspray and lipstick.

When it's our turn, the dancers and I take our places in the darkness. Then the lights come on. They're so bright I can feel the heat on my face. The audience is a blur. My heart is pounding.

I strum my fingers across the ukulele strings, lean into the microphone and start to sing.

The first chords of "A Day in the Life" jangle from the speakers. Claire and Nathalie get to their feet. They start to dance. They dance and dance. Their feet bounce to the beat and their arms sway wide. Nathalie's skirt twirls. Claire closes her eyes.

I sit with my arms wrapped around my knees. I want to join them but I can't. My body is glued to the floor.

I long to abandon myself to the music like they do. To feel the floorboards beneath my bare, dancing feet. To jump, to skip, to fly, fly high.

But I cannot move. The more I consider it, the more impossible it becomes. Nathalie dances over to me and offers her hand. I smile and shake my head. She shrugs, turns away again and takes Claire's hands. My insides tighten.

I hug my knees, watching, envy aching through me.

My amplified voice fills the auditorium. It echoes back to me like an estranged but welcome twin. The dancers' spins and jumps are met with whoops from the audience.

"*We're gonna rock, gonna rock, around the clock tonight.*"
And I truly do want to …

But time races forward and the song is already over. Claps and cheers erupt from the audience.

Afterward, my classmates congratulate me. They're surprised. They can't even picture themselves singing in public.

They don't understand. Singing is who I am. The only way I can express what's inside.

Gordon comes up to me. He holds out his hand. "Thanks," he says.

I stare at his outstretched arm. "For what?"

"Without you singing up there, I'd never have done this," he says. "I'd never have had the opportunity, or the courage, to get up on stage and dance."

Oh.

I reach out to shake his hand.
As I grasp his fingers, still hot
and sweaty from the dancing,
my head starts to spin.

And then I am whirling on the
dance floor.

I am whirling faster and faster,
until I fly right off. I am soaring beyond the school, flying
above the trees. Below, the cars
and people and houses are like
miniature toys on a carpet grid
of streets. For a moment, everything falls neatly into place.

Social Clues

Across

3. The next level in a friendship. You're beginning to realize this makes you uncomfortable, but you're not sure why.

4. Not together. Separated by distance.

7. That which ties two things, or two people, together. What you're lacking with others but not sure how to build.

9. How you feel sometimes when you are (see 5 down). Or sometimes when you are with other people but feel no (see 7 across).

10. The people who, apart from family, are most important to you. But sometimes you fear you have none who are close.

12. Power of comprehending. What you look for in people's eyes, in their words, for reassurance.

13. Opposite of "same."

15. What you were taught to do with your toys in kindergarten. What people do on Facebook. What you don't know how to do with your innermost thoughts and feelings.

17. What you long for when you see two people embrace. Third in Maslow's hierarchy of needs. What you want unconditionally. What you are ready to give.

Down

1. State of containing nothing. Feeling of something missing, lacking. Physical sensation that bores a hole in your gut.

2. Tied for third in Maslow's hierarchy of needs. What you crave when you see other people talking and laughing together.

5. By yourself, not with others. It's not always bad because sometimes you need your privacy, your autonomy, to spend time with your thoughts. But other times you feel this way in the world.

6. What you hoped for last week when you submitted a story to a literary journal. What you seek from other people.

8. Done or existing alone. One letter away from the card game. Two letters away from another word that means unity or mutual support within a group.

11. Physical suffering or discomfort caused by illness or injury. The dull ache that returns when you are left out, once again.

14. English rock band from the '80s: ____ for Fears. What you hide, what you shed at night on your pillow.

16. What springs eternal and what you cling to on the hardest of days.

Solution:

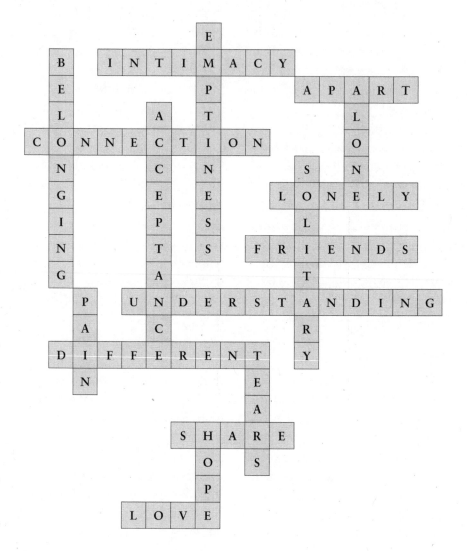

Carajillo

THICK, BITTERSWEET COFFEE wraps around my tongue. I swallow
and the hidden brandy warms my aching throat, tingling, lingering.

Adrenaline trumps my stress-induced congestion and exhaustion.

On the barstool beside me, my colleague, Colin, grins, bright eyes
looking directly into mine. I grin back. My husband Étienne spins an
anecdote about his first encounter with Spanish brandy.

But we can't stay long. We have to get back to the party. After all,
it's in honour of Étienne and me. Our last night in Barcelona. A year so
full. Plane tickets back to Canada bought on my credit card, invisible
money we do not have.

Tall, attentive, dark-haired Étienne, my other half. Together since
I was seventeen. My first, my only. This adventure is his idea. If not
for him, taking me by the hand, I'd never have experienced any of
this: living in a foreign country, away from what I know. Fire-breath-
ing dragon puppets and boys in bandanas taunting devils during the
Mercè. Human tower competitions in San Jaime square. Sweet, soft
ensaimada pastries. Spicy chorizo.

After a few months we found work as translators for a small
American-run newspaper. We made friends with the other staff, all En-
glish-speaking expats. Made friends as a couple. Étienne is quiet, too,
but knows how to start conversations. How to continue them, as well.

There's Gabriella, part Italian, part Swiss, long, curly black hair,
speaking five languages and always telling stories. In those weeks after
her break-up, she took refuge in our tiny apartment, her thin frame with-
ering even thinner. I was the helpful friend but Étienne was her lifeline.

There's lanky, angular-faced Jeremy from New Zealand. One night
he invited us to dinner. I marvelled at how from a bare fridge he

cooked up chicken gumbo overflowing onto baked potatoes. But it was Étienne who voiced the compliment.

Colin is from England. He is energetic, friendly and confident. Convincing in political debates. When he leans over my desk, Étienne watches.

At the party, people are talking in small groups, hands grasping bottles of cold beer. Étienne and I stand side by side. He excuses himself for a minute. Someone asks me a question and I panic. As always, my body grows hot, my mind goes blank. They are all watching me, waiting for my answer. I trip over my words. They nod and smile at me like I'm a child. Then someone makes a joke and everyone laughs. They turn back to each other with relief and resume the conversation.

My face continues to burn.

Colin nudges my shoulder and suggests we duck out to the bar across the street for a *carajillo*. I hesitate. He insists. I feel like a delinquent. But he's asking *me*. Not Étienne, me.

Who am I?

Colin takes my arm, sending a thrill shivering through my body.

Étienne is invited too, of course; we are a package. He follows as we slip out the door.

One afternoon a few weeks ago, while Étienne tutored some students in French, I wandered the streets of the Barrio Gótico.

It was the first time in months that I was on my own.

My feet wobbled over the uneven cobblestones. I stopped before the windows of antique shops, peering in at the clutter of wooden furniture, old dolls, chipped ceramic plates, empty picture frames and brass lamps. After a while I sat down at a bistro table outside a bar. I ordered an espresso in my still limited and limiting Spanish, or *castellano*—the sign of a foreigner in this Catalan city.

Students sauntered past with knapsacks slung over their shoulders. Women clicked by in their heels.

The waiter placed the coffee in front of me and left again, my "*Gracias*" and half-voiced request for a glass of water trailing after him. Resigned, I stirred in my packet of sugar.

Despite loving this place, this adventure, I was tired of struggling with the language. Interactions reduced to subject-verb-object. I was feeling stifled. Restless. Looking forward to the freedom of being back in Montreal.

Waiters weaved around me, clearing glasses and wiping tables with damp rags. Two small boys raced down the street shouting. Car horns blared. Smells of frying fish wafted from the restaurant next door. As I sat there, something began to tug at the edges of my consciousness.

My forearm brushed the cold metal of the chair and I glanced at my watch. Time to meet Étienne.

In the dimness of the bar, Colin's blond mane spreads around his face like an invitation. He asks what I will do after the plane lands. He scribbles his address on a scrap of paper. Then the three of us return to the party.

Many years later I will learn that *carajillo*, the Spanish drink combining coffee with brandy, whisky or rum, comes from the word *coraje*, meaning courage. It dates back to when Cuba was a Spanish colony, and the troops combined coffee with rum to give them courage.

Many years later, I will do something I could never have imagined on that day: I will leave Étienne to step out into the world on my own. People will say my decision took courage. But I will see it as the only way to discover who I really am.

The Master Class

I STAND STRAIGHT, toes feeling the textured weave of the carpet through my socks. Taking a deep breath and arranging my mouth in a neutral position, I repeat the sounds demonstrated by my singing teacher:

"*Nyam nyam nyam, nyoom nyoom nyoom.*"

From behind the piano, Chantale nods. "So remember," she says in French, "keep the middle of your tongue flat against the upper palate, without applying pressure. And open your nasal passages to let the sound resonate."

She plays a low G and I "*nyam nyam*" up the scale, slowly, and then back down again.

"Good," she says, and begins the next scale. This time I "*nyoom.*" We continue in this way for five or six scales, starting a halftone higher each time.

As I concentrate on the shape my mouth is making, I gaze out the window behind Chantale, fixing a point on a streetlamp. My hands shift from my sides to behind my back to clasped in front of me.

It's only ten minutes into the lesson and already I'm sweating, wetness spreading under my arms. It doesn't matter what the season is or what I'm wearing. I always sweat. Partly it's the effort of concentration. Mostly it's the act of standing in front of Chantale. I feel naked and exposed.

It's the same story every week.

I've been singing for as long as I can remember. When I was a child, my family would attend musicals put on by the local theatre troupe near our country house across the border in Vermont, and I'd come home with the songs already memorized. In Grade 2, I joined my elementary school choir, rehearsing at lunch hour and performing at Christmas and end-of-year events. In high school, I sang in talent shows.

The thing is, singing has always been my saving grace. In elementary school, I was incredibly timid. In high school, I'd blush if a boy so much as glanced my way. Singing in those talent shows was the one way I could escape my shy, awkward, bumbling self. I've always jumped at the chance to be on stage.

Singing is my way of expressing myself. Music conveys feeling much more easily than plain words. And with singing, I know exactly what to do. There's a score that I've memorized and practised. Unlike navigating the unpredictable, unrehearsed world of human interactions, singing is something I understand and know how to do.

At least, I thought I did. About three years ago, I decided to fulfill a lifelong dream and take lessons. It's certainly not a decision I regret. My voice is becoming fuller and stronger, my range has expanded, and I've been introduced to all kinds of music—classical, liturgical, opera, contemporary. But it's one of those things where the more you learn, the more you realize how little you know.

For one thing, I'd never realized how physical singing is. I'm not so good with stuff that involves the body. I tried jazz ballet once in my late teens. I was put in a beginner class with ten-year-olds. I could barely swivel my hips, let alone keep up with the teacher's complicated choreographies. The younger kids pranced around me, giggling. It was awful.

Chantale ties her brown hair into a ponytail with a scrunchie as she describes the next exercise, "yo" and "ya." Keeping the tip of my tongue against the inside of my bottom teeth, I'm to raise the back of my tongue as much as possible. She demonstrates. I repeat. We start again at low G and go up and down each scale, alternating between "yo" and "ya."

It's always the same series of exercises, each one designed to develop a different combination of muscles. Yet somehow, each time, she emphasizes a different aspect, gives it a different nuance. Or maybe there's something she's been saying for months, but one day it clicks. It suddenly makes sense, because my body is ready for it.

We pause for a break. I take a sip from my water bottle.

"So how do you find living with roommates?" Chantale asks.

I picture my sunny bedroom overlooking busy St. Denis Street. I've been living there for two months, since my break-up. I think about blond-haired Isabelle, a Master's student from France. The other day she prepared a zucchini omelet for us to share and we sat in the kitchen getting to know each other. I think of Dana collapsing on the sofa after roller-blading home from her job teaching English to immigrants, and how we've developed a ritual of opening a bottle of wine and watching *Law & Order* together on TV.

"It's good," is all I say to Chantale.

"Do you have rules, like about who does the dishes?" she asks.

"Not really. Not yet." A fair question though. Isabelle complains that Dana leaves dirty dishes lying around the apartment. For me, everything is still too new and exciting for a few empty mugs on the coffee table to matter.

Chantale chuckles. "I've had my share of crazy roommates. So glad to be on my own now. Okay, next exercise ..."

I don't know a whole lot about Chantale. She's at least five years older than me. She has a twelve-year-old daughter who lives with her, but I gather the father has been out of the picture for years. Besides teaching, Chantale sings professionally with the Opéra de Montréal and a few other groups—it varies according to the season's repertoire.

For "*du du, do do,*" she reminds me to keep my feet planted, rooted like a tree in the ground. I elongate my spine. The sound begins in my chest and vibrates up to the top of my head, reaching for the sky.

I didn't pick Isabelle and Dana; they picked me. After visiting a dozen different places, I was debating between their room and somewhere else and was about to take the somewhere else (quieter street, lower monthly rent) when Dana called.

"We're wondering if you've made a decision about the room," she said. "We've interviewed a bunch of people, but you're our first choice."

Up to that point I guess I'd mostly been looking at the rooms, not really considering the people in them.

I immediately called the other people back and told them I was no longer interested.

After the next exercise, Chantale asks, "Do you miss him?"

"Him" being my former partner of ten-plus years.

I don't. Honestly. By the time I left the relationship, all feelings of romantic love were gone. I still care about him, but ... not in that way. I do miss being in a relationship. But I also enjoy the freedom of not being in one. Of not having to consult anyone to make decisions. Not having to consider anyone else in the equation. Doing whatever I want to do. It's intoxicating.

After the exercises, we move on to the piece I've been working on: "Voi che sapete," in which a young page describes the trials of first love. It's from Mozart's opera *The Marriage of Figaro*. Lately Chantale has been giving me opera arias like this to get me to sing out, full voice, in preparation for our spring recital. This will be the first one where I'm on my own. That is, no boyfriend in the audience to support me unconditionally and cheer me on.

"Will you invite your roommates?" Chantale asks at one point.

Maybe. Maybe not. I haven't decided.

After three years, I've gotten used to her questions. I suspect these breaks are not simply to give my muscles a few minutes to relax, but also to get to know me. Because standing there trying to sing ... it's hard to describe. Your emotional self is laid bare. It's no coincidence that, during those breaks, I find myself telling her things about my personal life that I haven't told anyone else.

She lets me sing through the whole piece once—she always insists, even if I'm struggling—before giving her comments and going back to work on specific sections. Today, we spend several minutes on a part where I have to sing at an uncomfortable register—not because it's exceptionally high or low, but because it's in between. It's where I switch from chest voice to head voice, known as "*le passage*" (the transition) in French, and in English as "the break." No doubt because it's usually the weakest part of a person's range, where the voice often cracks.

Ideally, you want to carry the brilliance of the head voice into your chest voice, and the depth and resonance of the chest voice into your head voice. The *passage* should be a mix of the two. This blend gives you a full and even voice.

But I'm not there yet. In fact, I've been struggling with this for a while.

"It's as if something is blocking you, holding you back," Chantale comments.

Story of my life, I think.

She tilts her head and looks at me.

I shrug and force a smile.

Suddenly she claps the music book shut. "Let's try something new."

Uh-oh. I've come to dread it when she says that. "Something new" can mean anything, from sight-reading an obscure piece of early music to lying on a foam roller doing Pilates breathing.

But it's not so bad this time. She wants me to sing "*ah*" sliding up and down an octave, slowly and smoothly, leaving my throat open and relaxed. When I get to the *passage*, she has me narrow the sound to just a thread; she wants me to move to the next note as if I'm threading a needle, carefully, without any break.

I try. I'm sweating again. I don't know where to put my hands. I shift from foot to foot. I feel like a crooked tomato plant, overgrown and in need of support.

"I'll practise it when I get home," I say.

She shakes her head. "Try it now."

It's a familiar exchange: I want to take it away and do it in private. She insists that I practise in front of her, right away, right here, right now. There's no way out. Deep down I know she's right, because otherwise I may not practise it properly ... or at all. But that doesn't make it easier.

Sometimes, I can't help feeling that she's putting me on the spot. Deliberately. Like how once at a restaurant after a choir concert, when she suggested the whole group play a game taking turns to make up a story. I took the suggestion as my cue to leave, and was just reaching for my coat, when she shouted out my name. She insisted that I start the game. I froze. My mind went blank. I mumbled an excuse, but she wouldn't drop it. By the time I left the restaurant, the entire choir was chanting my name. Beneath my tears of mortification, I was furious. Extroverts seem to think that what shy people need is to be forced to do things, out in the open. It's not that simple.

But this is a private lesson. She and I are alone. I am paying her to teach me.

I try again. I push through the discomfort, my face hot.

She nods. "Keep working on that. It'll make a difference. You'll see."

It's a damp Sunday afternoon in April. Rain splatters the old-fashioned mullioned windows of the small auditorium in the former convent that is now the Vincent d'Indy music school.

Once a month, Chantale holds a master class here for her students. We take turns performing our pieces. After each performance, Chantale works with us individually for a few minutes in front of the other students. Sometimes she asks the audience questions. We learn as much from watching each other as we do from our own time on the stage.

It's my turn. I make my way to the front of the room.

My knees start to wobble. My gait becomes uneven. The room is much longer than I remember. There's a throbbing in my ears, which I suddenly realize is the sound of my own blood coursing through my veins. A dozen pairs of eyes follow my every movement.

When I started voice lessons, it was different. The instant I started singing, my nervousness would dissipate and I could just sing. That doesn't happen anymore. Not really. It's as if the more I learn, the more I expect of myself—the higher the stakes, the farther I have to fall.

Earlier in the class, Chantale tried to get the first student, André, to stop moving around so much. Agitation is a flaw common to most of us. You can tell which parts of the piece are the most difficult by how much the person moves. It's like we compensate for what we can't do with our voices by doing it with our bodies. Chantale had André start over every time he moved a finger. At first he kept bursting out laughing, and so did we, because he couldn't get through a single phrase. But then he started to concentrate, and soon we were all amazed. His voice turned rich and pure, merely by keeping his body (his instrument, Chantale reminded us) straight and still. It focused his energy and allowed the sound to flow free, rather than cutting it off like a bent straw.

With Geneviève, Chantale worked on mental imagery. What was the setting for the song? The mood? She directed Geneviève to close her eyes. Was she inside a house in the city, or outside in the country? Was she in a forest, a meadow, or by a lake? Was it day or night? What season? What did the air smell like? Once Geneviève had a clear image in her mind, she opened her eyes and sang the aria again. It was entirely different. The music had come to life, a seemingly random set of notes transformed into story.

I mount the stairs to the stage. Even though it's just class and not a public performance, my heart is pounding fast and hard in my chest. Right about now is when I always ask myself, why do I put myself through this? Why do I torture myself?

I ask myself the same questions every time I'm about to interview someone for an article. I have to take deep breaths before picking up the phone so that it doesn't sound like I've just run a marathon. Why did I, a person who isn't particularly skilled at talking to people and asking questions, choose journalism as a vocation? That fateful day when I applied to the university's journalism program, what was I thinking?

But I know exactly what I was thinking. It was a career in which I'd able to write and express myself. My way of changing the world. And it would force me to go beyond my comfort zone and interact with people. The byline was my reward: a published article was akin to a public performance.

Which is why I participate in these master classes. It's all very fine to blend in with a choir and be one of many. There's a thrill in being part of an ensemble, an exhilaration in contributing to produce the mass of sound required for a crescendo or the intricate weaving of parts for the polyphony of a fugue. But there is no denying the ego rush that comes from singing solo. From standing out from the crowd.

I'm finally in position on the stage. I nod at the pianist, who starts to play. I take a breath and open my mouth.

I stumble on a few notes, but I make it all the way through "Voi che sapete" without any major mishaps. When I'm finished everyone claps as usual, and then I stand there waiting to hear what Chantale will say. My body feels awkward. I avoid looking at the faces in the audience and focus on the teacher at the back of the room. A few people turn in their seats, also waiting for her to speak.

She is silent for what feels like minutes but is probably only seconds. I try not to shift from foot to foot. Once again, my face is hot and dampness is spreading under my arms.

"What do you think is missing?" she asks the group.

A chair squeaks. Someone takes a swig of water. A pencil scratches paper.

A girl raises her hand. "Maybe she could sing louder?"

Does that mean they can't hear me? It seemed loud enough to me, but maybe my voice doesn't carry like I imagine. What we hear in our own heads is often not what others hear.

"Maybe she can try not moving around so much, like André?" someone else suggests.

True, I do move around. Not as much as André, but still.

"I'd like to try something," Chantale says.

Uh-oh. But maybe this will be like the "*ah*" scale at my lesson. I can do that.

Chantale gets up and walks to the front of the room where I'm standing. She has me place my feet a bit apart, one in front of the other in a warrior stance. Then she stretches my arms up and out, opening my chest.

For someone who has spent her whole life hunched over and curled up into herself, this is the most uncomfortable position imaginable. It goes against all my instincts. I have to fight every natural impulse just to maintain it.

Chantale tells the pianist to start the piece. Then to me: "Go ahead. Sing."

I begin. "*Voi che sapete che cosa è amor, donne, vedete, s'io l'ho nel cor ...*"

My shoulders start to slump. Chantale tugs my arms back up and out. "Keep going."

"*Donne, vedete, s'io l'ho nel cor.*"

"Shoulders back! Arms out! Spread your fingers!"

"*Quello ch'io provo, vi ridirò; è per me nuovo, capir nol so ...*"

My whole body is vibrating, humming. And then, the sound rushes forth, breaking free, like water pouring through an open gate.

"*Sento un affetto pien di desir, ch'ora è diletto, ch'ora è martir ...*"

My voice fills the room. I am floating, untethered.

"*Gelo, e poi sento l'alma avvampar, e in un momento torno a gelar.*

"*Ricerco un bene fuori di me — non so chi il tiene, non so cos'è.*"

I am high up on a tightrope without a harness. Flying down a roller coaster without a seat belt. I struggle not to panic. Sound is pouring out of me like a vessel emptying.

"Sospiro e gemo senza voler; palpito e tremo senza saper,

"Non trovo pace notte nè dì, ma pur mi piace languir così ..."

"Go, go, go!" Chantale shouts.

"Voi, che sapete che cosa è amor, donne, vedete, s'io l'ho nel cor; donne, vedete, s'io l'ho nel cor; donne, vedete, s'io l'ho nel cor!"

By the time I arrive at the end of the song, my head is spinning.

The room erupts in cheers. Chantale lets me put my arms down and I slink back to my seat. All around me people are talking excitedly. I'm aware of Chantale's voice, but I can't focus on what she's saying. My insides feel like they've been scooped out. I am exhausted.

Eventually, the next student takes the stage, and I sit dutifully watching and listening.

I am astounded at what my voice can do. It is a breakthrough. But what I want most at this moment is to curl into a ball, away from everyone, and let the tears flow.

There would be many more years of lessons, master classes and recitals.

What I would come to realize is that art and life cannot exist on separate planes. It's not about art imitating life or life imitating art. The two are intertwined. They feed and fuel each other. Chantale understood this. She believed in the power to make things happen, in music and in life. She believed in me.

I stand straight, toes feeling the textured weave of the carpet through my socks. I plant my feet on the ground. Taking a deep breath, I begin to climb up the scale.

PART II
VOICES LOST

Between the Rows

MY MOTHER SHOWED ME how to plant peas when I was six years old: make a row of holes in the earth with your finger ("up to the second joint"), about an inch apart. Drop in the seeds, little white pills. Cover them and gently pack the earth. We'd water them and a week or two later, there would be little sprouts poking through the earth, tiny stems with tiny leaves.

We lived in the city, but on weekends and during summer vacation we'd escape to the country house my father had built. That's where the garden was. A land of barns and hay silos and tractors and cows. The smell of fresh manure permeated the car as we drove past fertilized fields. Gravel crunched under the wheels when we turned down our driveway.

My mother would set to pulling out the weeds that had flourished during the week. Some were as tall as the vegetable plants themselves, stretching their stems and flaunting their leaves as they sought to choke out their rivals.

"Up to the second joint." To be honest, although I remember the words, I can't remember her voice. She died when I was ten years old. When I replay my memories, I don't know what voice to give her.

My father sold the country house a few years ago. He was in his late seventies. His health had deteriorated and he could no longer make the drive. While packing, sorting and culling books, my step-mom found a hardbound notebook with a blank cover. She handed it to me without explanation.

I opened to the first page.

A shiver started at the back of my neck, travelled down my arms, brushed my skin. My mother's handwriting.

I flipped the pages one by one.

The musty scent of old paper rose as I fingered the smooth corners.

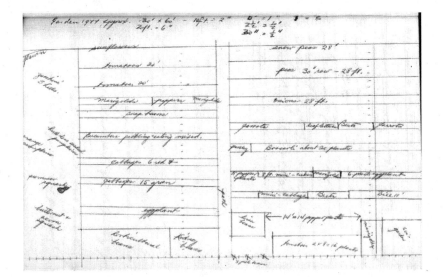

A gardening journal. Seed varieties and quantities. What had worked and what hadn't.

My mother had also drawn plans. They reminded me of my father's architectural drawings, all straight lines and square edges. Was she always this methodical? Maybe she'd read an article in a magazine about keeping a log.

There weren't many entries. Most were brief: notes on whether the plants got too much rain or too much sun or were eaten by bugs, and how much was harvested. But after a while, the entries became more descriptive, mentioning a day trip she and my father took to Morrisville, weekend guests, who planted what.

And then I saw my name. My heart leapt.

> May 27/79 Eve, Steph me down for day.
> Watered seedlings.
> Planted 8 celery plants / 2 Pixie Tom. (Eve)
> parsley & parsnip from seedlings (Eve)
> 4 savoy cabbage
> weeded strawberries.
> Spread bed of dried blood around peas & lettu...
> Lots of rain last week. Rained tonight + last night.

She was talking about me.

How does handwriting convey voice? How does it embody a soul?

There's an intimacy. As if the ink has flowed directly from the person's heart, through their arm and hand, and onto the page.

Somewhere in the slant of the writing, the crossed-out words and the spaces between the rows of script, I'd found the voice I was looking for.

I picture my mother in the vegetable garden, in her brown tank top and wide-brimmed hat, sun beating down on her arms as she bends over to pull out weeds. Face serene, lost in thought.

In winter she'd sit at the dining room table poring over seed catalogues, circling varieties and taking notes. She'd start the seedlings indoors—tomatoes, peppers, celery. My father built her a rack with special lights. As soon as it was dry enough in the spring, she'd get my father to plow the patch with the garden tiller. It got a little bigger each time.

I had my own little patch in the corner. I planted carrots, lettuce and radishes. Cherry tomatoes, too. We marked out the rows with wooden stakes and string, just like in the big garden. But mine became overgrown with weeds very quickly.

I was more interested in roaming the field of tall grass at the bottom of the garden. It may have been hay or straw, but I called it oats, because the tops reminded me of the picture of oat branches on my morning Cheerios box. Toward the end of the summer, the stalks were taller than I was. I'd step through and they'd close behind me like a curtain, swallowing me whole. I'd try to run, laughing at the impossibility of it, and then let myself fall. The stalks would catch me, bending back to form a thick cushion, the dry ones poking at the skin on my arms and legs. I'd lie there listening to grasshoppers flitting and bees buzzing, and stare up at the blue, blue sky.

After a while I'd return to the garden. My mother would still be there, weeding. She'd pause to push her glasses up with the back of an earth-covered hand. By this time of year, the rows of the garden would be leafy and full, prickly cucumbers poking out from giant dusty leaves, tomato plants bending with the weight of ripening fruit, string beans dangling.

After a rainfall, my mother would caution: "Never pick beans while the plants are still wet. They'll get a disease."

Funny, the odd bits you remember.

Mirrors

"YOUR AUNT RUTH has passed away."

The news comes as a shock. Well, not entirely. I knew she was sick. I just hadn't realized the cancer was so far along, that it had taken over.

"The funeral is on Sunday at 11, at Paperman's," the caller, a close family friend, says. She has to give me the exact address because I am probably the only Jew in Montreal who has no idea where the Paperman & Sons funeral home is.

I put down the phone and stare out my apartment window at the building opposite. The same four-storey red-brick building that stands there as always, impassive, filling up most of my window, leaving just a strip of white December sky.

My aunt Ruth has died.

A few snowflakes drift past the brick wall. It was a school once, decades ago, but has since been turned into condos.

I hadn't seen much of my aunt these last few years. The real shock, as always, was the diagnosis. But now, she is the third person in my world to die of breast cancer: first, my mother, when I was ten; then, my best friend's mother, not three years ago; now Ruth, wife of my father's brother.

The flakes are big and fluffy, melting as soon as they touch the sidewalk. It's not quite winter yet.

When I was little, on nights up at the country house, I loved to stick my head out the door when it was snowing, and stare up at the white flakes falling from the black sky. The sky was so much darker in the country. If I positioned myself just so, with nothing else in my line of sight—just the white flakes falling—I could feel myself being pulled up, up into the night. It was like falling upward. It was like travelling through space, the flakes white stars in the void, like in a *Star Wars* movie. They would land and melt on my forehead, cheeks and nose, cold, wet, soft. Eventually I would get dizzy, or have to blink because there was snow in my eye, and the spell would be broken.

I think of my two cousins, Rachel and Danielle. We are strangers who meet once a year at family gatherings. Actually, I don't think I've seen them for a few years. I calculate: I've just turned 30, so Rachel must be 21, and Danielle, 19. Is there an age when it becomes easier to lose a mother?

I move through the rest of the day as planned, working, making phone calls, eating meals. But the day is tinged with a sense of something fundamental having been altered, the image the same, yet not quite as trustworthy. Question marks hang over every gesture, every object, like halos, and I wonder if anyone else can see them, and if they have always been there.

My sister will be driving up from Kingston directly, so I'll meet her at the funeral. My father and my step-mom are travelling in California. They're not sure they'll find a flight to make it back here in time.

The night before the service, I suddenly wonder if there is something I am supposed to do. What is expected of me? What is appropriate? A card? It's after 7 p.m. as I head down St. Laurent Street. Restaurant windows glow as people sit down to wine with friends, but most of the shop fronts have their gates pulled. Luckily, the poster store is still open. I search the rows of cards for something neutral. A landscape, maybe. Finally I settle on a Monet, blue trees reflected in water, the indistinct brushstrokes swirling reality and reflection into one, the whole shrouded in fog.

Wandering back through the dark winter streets, pulling my coat and scarf closer around my neck against the chill, I wonder what to write. I imagine an angry Danielle tearing up stock sympathy cards, and an older, pragmatic Rachel appealing to her not to and crying into the night.

No words will fill the void. All I can do is offer them my love, and hope they will feel comfortable calling me if they need something. Early the next morning, after a night of restless dreams seeping in through the edges of my consciousness, that is what I write.

After losing half an hour fretting over what to wear, and then forgetting that it's Sunday and the buses are on a slower schedule, I arrive at the Paperman & Sons funeral parlour late. It is a place of dark panelled wood and polished brass handles and soft beige carpets. Everything is very tidy and tasteful and impersonal and quiet. Very quiet.

I sign a sheet with the heading "Family and Friends," and then hesitate, looking at the yarmulkes piled for the men and the kerchiefs for the women. I know men are supposed to cover their heads in the synagogue, but what is the rule for women—only married women? I try desperately to remember. I take a chance and go in bareheaded.

There are more people at the service than I had expected. More than Paperman's had expected as well, because later my sister tells me that they had started in the small chapel, but then with people standing in the back and more still coming, they had to move everyone into the larger room. I slip into a pew at the back.

After a few minutes of silence, a man rolls the coffin into the room, followed by the ... Rabbi? It is a she. She addresses the congregation, and her words are not impersonal or indifferent as I had feared. She sings a prayer (perhaps she is a Cantor?), and the singing reconciles me with this place, this ceremony. Then she invites one of Ruth's friends, and then Ruth's sister, to speak.

Listening to the eulogies, I feel like a stranger. I realize I barely knew my aunt. She is described as courageous, determined, always going out of her way to help people. A sister who would save up money to take her siblings to the movies. A teacher who remembered the names and faces of all her students years later. A wife intent on keeping a proper home. A mother who was always clipping articles and finding new activities for her daughters.

To close the ceremony, the Rabbi reads two hymns selected by "the children," who are sitting hidden from view. The first asks God to take care of she who has departed; the second asks God to give strength to those left behind.

At the cemetery, gathered around the grave, I see my cousins at last. They are so thin. They stand at the foot of the grave beside the Rabbi, long dark coats flapping around their legs. Danielle, slightly shorter, has a wide-brimmed hat pulled down almost over her eyes. Rachel stands tall, face and head bare to the bitter wind, her raw grief exposed to the eyes of all who stand there. She is trembling with her choked tears. The wind tangles her long hair. Her arm is fast around Danielle. My uncle stands apart, slightly behind them. There were problems between him and his wife in the last year. He even moved out for a while. Has her death brought him relief? Freedom? Loneliness? Despair? It's impossible to tell.

The Rabbi/Cantor begins to sing, and although I cannot understand the words, it is not the first time that I think Hebrew is a perfect language for singing. Her voice is the phoenix rising from sorrow.

The prayer ends. The echo of the music (what is more alive and ephemeral than music?) dies in the wind.

They begin to recite the Kaddish. Rachel's voice grows louder as she clings to the words for strength. She is now the woman of the house.

The whipping of the cold. The hard ground, frozen in lumps under our feet. Rachel, trembling or praying, I can't tell. A moment. Then, she nods, and the coffin is lowered into the grave.

Danielle and Rachel clinging to each other: that image, their grief, forever, standing still in time.

Handfuls of earth are tossed into the grave, as is the custom. A brief memory: someone telling me to throw a handful of earth into the grave, onto my mother's coffin. Obeying. Numb. I couldn't cry.

Shiva, the seven days of mourning where family and friends come to console the bereaved, is traditionally held at the family home. Realization hits me when I pull up outside the familiar bungalow.

Until that moment, while my cousins' grief was very real, it seemed to belong in a sphere of its own. A funeral, a burial, these are rituals where you are really just an observer. But a familiar gesture, pulling the car up outside the house I have entered hundreds of times and realizing that Ruth will not be there to greet me, will never greet me again—that is the moment of loss.

I have been coming to this house since I was a little girl, and always, upon ringing the bell and entering, Ruth has appeared. Sometimes Rachel would answer, but my aunt was never far behind, calling from the kitchen, hurrying over while wiping her hands on a dish towel, ushering us in, directing us to put our coats on the bed in the master bedroom.

I believe that is the hardest part: making ourselves believe we will never see the person again. I say "believe" because the truth is simply not believable. After my mother's death, I had dreams where the doorbell would ring and I would open the door, and there would be my mother.

When I was in Grade 2, my aunt Ruth taught Grade 5 in the same school. Her students would say hello to me in the hall and I would have no idea who they were. Sometimes she would call me into her classroom, and I would feel both shy and proud. Once, while her students were busy working at their desks, she sent for me and pulled out a chain of rings, trying them on my finger to find the right size. That year for my birthday she and my uncle gave me a gold ring with a red stone in the middle. I wore it for years until it became too small.

What I remember most are the Passover Seders. Ruth would preside over them in her teacher-like manner, trying to get through the whole ceremony before my uncle and my father became too impatient to start the meal. Rachel and Danielle participated eagerly and dutifully, getting upset whenever my uncle tried to skip over a part in the ritual. The ceremony did get more condensed as the years went by, my aunt handing out new and revised versions of the Haggadah each time. The meal was always hearty and good, mostly catered—gefilte fish with horseradish on a plate of salad, matzo-ball soup, brisket, chicken, gravy, candied carrots, potato kugel, pickles, and plenty of *haroset*. Between the two families we must have been about fifteen people, and Ruth was always very anxious that everyone be served and have enough to eat and not wait too long for their tea and coffee. She would hire kitchen help to ensure that everything went smoothly.

There were years when going to the Passover Seder was an obligation to be fulfilled rather than something I looked forward to. Now I realize it was the only link I had left to my culture and heritage, and the only real family gatherings we had.

I climb the steps slowly. The door is unlocked. Rachel comes over as I pull off my boots, with her characteristic polite "Thank you for coming." It's the same greeting as when we used to come for Passover, and which always made it seem like she was acting too old for her age. Except this time there is a hug, and her body feels like a fragile reed in my arms. Danielle looks on from behind her. Both in black, identical scarves wrapped around their necks. They are a year and a half apart in age. Rachel is taller and has always struck me as the socially correct, take-charge type who knows what she wants. Danielle is smaller and has always seemed more insecure, stubborn and rebellious. Yet they are inseparable. It is possible they now feel they have only each other in the world.

We catch up on superficial news. Rachel is in medical school at McGill and Danielle is in her first year of commerce at Concordia. Rachel loves the program. Danielle likes commerce but is thinking of switching to Queen's next year. She was accepted this year but decided not to go because of her mother's illness. Maybe next year. They are willing to transfer her credits.

Then I see my uncle moving across the room. My eyes take in his unsteady walk, his haggard face, the ripped tie, and I am brought back twenty years, seeing my father in his place.

Hard low chairs for the mourners. Mirrors covered. People will bring cooked meals in containers wrapped in plastic bags or send baskets of food. I am surprised how much comes back to me.

When my mother was alive, we kept up the traditions. We lit candles and sang the prayer on Chanukah, each of the eight nights. I still remember the prayer: "*Barou ha-tah Adonai, elohanou melehaoulum.*" All sounds, because I never learned Hebrew. I don't know when we stopped lighting the candles. Was it when she died, or was it when we grew up and became a part of the modern Christian world around us?

My parents would keep us home on the High Holidays, but we never fasted or went to synagogue. As if the tradition was too ingrained to have us go to school, but their belief not strong enough to bring us to synagogue. Images remain in my mind: my mother chopping prunes to make *hamantashen* on Purim. Squirming impatiently in my seat during the interminable Passover Seders my grandfather led at our house, the whole story in Hebrew first and then again in English so that we would understand. I remember one year hunting for the *afikoman* he had hid, and finding instead a piece of matzah I'd made at school, and thinking it was the funniest thing in the world.

That was my one year at a Jewish school: kindergarten. There, we celebrated all the holidays, dressed up at Purim, formed a singing human menorah on Chanukah, visited a sukkah on Sukkot. I learned the Hebrew words for mother and father (which I have since forgotten). I learned how to write my Jewish name, Chava, in Hebrew (since forgotten as well). I vaguely recall the stories of the Maccabees restoring the temple, and of Moses parting the waters of the Red Sea.

Then I switched to our local public elementary school, and I was pretty much the only Jew in the school.

At my aunt's house, I wander through the maze of people, feeling both as if I belong and as if I do not. It is all so familiar, and yet part of another life. Nearly everyone here is Jewish. This is the world I grew up in but have drifted away from. I recognize the parts, but not the whole. Relatives who I haven't seen since I was a child come over and reintroduce themselves—"I'm Alan, Ruth's brother. Remember? I dropped by your parents' country house once when I was on a bike trip and showed you how to press flowers and make rice paper lamps. This is my wife, Judy. We're living in Chicago now."

"We should buy up all the land around it and plant trees," Danielle says, holding the fridge door open so that Rachel can rearrange the contents to make room for the food people have brought. They are talking about the cemetery where their mother is now buried. It has become so full that it is no longer a peaceful park, just rows and rows and rows of tombstones, in our desperate attempt to remember every person that has been.

My sister and I have been wondering since this afternoon: is that the cemetery where our mother is buried? I wonder if, like me, this has been a question on the edge of her mind for the past few years. I have never dared to ask my father. At the time I was too young to think about where the line of cars was carrying us, and we never went back as a family. My uncle now solves the mystery: our mother is buried in Dollard-des-Ormeaux. I am disappointed, because that is more difficult for me to get to. But I feel better knowing.

54

I recognize more than the covered mirrors and the ripped tie; I recognize the atmosphere. The energy that normally inhabits a room full of people is sucked up by the black hole of my aunt's absence. People talk and joke, but there is a subdued tone, the unspoken hanging at every silence. Snatches of conversation drift and hover, like swirls of smoke:

"… before her time …"

"… too young …"

"… a good life …"

As I watch Rachel and Danielle, I know that all this—this day, this house full of people, this conversation, this chair they sit on—is not real to them. It is impossible to imagine that life will become livable again. There is an emptiness that no amount of talking or running or writing will fill.

Loud exclamations of greetings suddenly ring out and I turn to see my cousin Wendy in the doorway. Cheeks flushed, long wavy hair spilling over her coat, all warmth and hugs and smiles as everyone bustles around her. Though she has the slightly harried look of having just gotten off a plane. The room seems to brighten as she shifts her nine-month-old baby to one hip to embrace Rachel. The baby watches with big eyes as she chews on a strand of her mother's hair.

Danielle gently tugs the baby's tiny sock-covered foot. "Hello little girl!" The baby gives her a big smile, waves her arms and legs and starts to babble.

That night lying in bed, I stare at the ceiling in the dark. I can no longer avoid it, the thing that has been lurking in the back of my mind since the moment I heard the news about my aunt: I am terrified of death. I am terrified by the thought of non-existence, of no longer "being," for all eternity; no consciousness anymore, ever. It seems selfish to admit that this is what has bothered me most these past three days. It seems cowardly to wish that I had been brought up in a more religious household so that I would believe in God and not have this fear. Do Rachel and Danielle believe in an afterlife? Judaism is vague on this point.

I jump up and switch on the light, wishing to blind my fear out of existence.

I make myself a mug of chamomile tea and open the back door. Cold air gusts into the room. The frozen garden is silent. It's the first time I have an apartment with a garden. I wonder if there will be crocuses in the spring. I should have asked the previous tenant. I should have planted some. Aren't you supposed to plant them in the fall? I love the way crocuses poke through in the spring, green and alive, the first signs of life after the bleakness of winter.

The image of Wendy's baby at the shiva comes into my head: her big eyes, the way she smiled and wriggled her arms and legs, trying to answer with her whole body when Danielle said hello. The way the room brightened.

It has started to snow again. I put down my mug. I thrust my head out the door into the cold damp air, cup my hands around my eyes to block out the city lights and buildings, and stare up into the white flakes falling from the night.

Lost: Morris Listowel Piano, circa 1915

Contains: Unrealized dreams. If found, please play.

WHEN I WAS GROWING UP, we had an old piano in our living room. It was a full upright, with dark brown wood, ivory keys, and a loose, full sound. The middle C was chipped, which made it easy to find when I was learning to play.

It was a player piano, and when I was little it still worked. I loved to watch the keys go up and down. I'd open up the front panels to see the paper scroll turning, its punched-out holes rotating in patterns. It worked with compressed air: two foot pedals folded out from a sliding panel in the base. You had to pump them to keep the piano going.

Over the years the tubing for the player mechanism began to dry, falling out in pieces until it was beyond repair. But it was a great piano. I played it all through my childhood, composed songs on it, and used it to accompany my singing.

When my dad and my step-mom sold their house, my childhood home, I made some inquiries about getting the piano restored and moving it to my place. But it wasn't considered a particularly good make and, because it was a player piano, it weighed a ton. I was living in a small apartment at the time. When my dad mentioned he'd had to reinforce the floor to support the piano's weight, I gave up. My parents sold it.

If I'd known what I know now, I'd have never let it go.

I'm sitting on a sofa in my uncle's bungalow in Saint-Lazare, a suburb just off the western tip of the island of Montreal. My uncle David settles his six-foot-plus frame comfortably onto the other side. Now in his early seventies, his movements are slow, deliberate, unhurried.

Perhaps he always moved that way: always in control, always gentle, speaking in a measured voice, with a laugh coming right from his belly.

On the floor before us lies the reason for my visit: two large cardboard boxes overflowing with old family photographs and newspaper clippings chronicling my grandfather's involvement in the Jewish community when he was young. I'm here in search of his stories, hoping to fill the gaps in what I know. I'm here to learn about my roots.

My uncle takes the items out one by one. He studies them through his thick glasses, his dark bushy brows furrowing as he tries to figure out who is who, what is what. There are stacks of pictures, black and white, in various sizes. A few are in cardboard frames: my mother as a little girl. My grandparents on their wedding day. My grandfather in his late twenties, in a formal pose with two other young men. In one picture he leans proudly against a car, a Ford Model T, from his job as a travelling salesman.

David hands me a copy of *The Canadian Jewish Chronicle* from November 7, 1930. It's in tabloid format with the tagline, "The first and foremost Anglo-Jewish Weekly in Canada—Successor to the Canadian Jewish Times, Founded in 1897." Coincidentally, that was the year of my grandfather's birth in Russia. On page 10 is my grandparents' engagement announcement. On page 3, an article by Winston Churchill about Palestine.

Other miscellaneous items include: a balance sheet for my grandfather's company, S. & K. Clothing Inc., for the fiscal year 1929–1930 (net loss: $518.89). A five-page speech, typed on legal-size paper with the occasional correction handwritten in ink, which my grandfather delivered at the eighth annual convention of the "Zionist Order Habonim." My uncle's and mother's school report cards, signed by their mother.

Whenever I used to see my uncle David, he'd hug me and ask, "How's the writing going?" He knew I wanted to be a writer. As a kid I was always writing short stories, poems and songs. But as a young adult, my reaction to his question became one of recurring guilt. I knew I should be trying harder. Sure, I was writing some newspapers articles, but that's not what he meant. I'd complain that "real" work (i.e., paid work) always got in the way.

So when I first called David to tell him I wanted to write a story about my grandfather, I thought he'd be thrilled.

He wasn't.

"We were never close," he explained, in his distinctive deep voice. My grandfather was forty-four when David was born. It was too big a gap. He didn't understand the life of a Canadian teenager. Even though he grew up in Canada, it was within an immigrant community that kept to the old ways. "Society changed. He never adapted," my uncle said.

Now, photos and newspaper clippings spread out before us on a basement table, David tells me what he knows.

Abraham Aube Katz was born in 1897 in the town of Dinovitz, near Kamenetz-Podolsk, in Russia. The area, which later became part of the Ukraine, was in the "Pale of Settlement," the territory where Russian Jews were forced to live.

In 1907, when Abe was ten, his family fled the pogroms, bringing him and his three sisters to Montreal. His father opened a butcher shop on Roy Street. Around age thirteen, Abe left school to work in the shop and help his father deliver packages of meat in a horse-driven wagon.

At some point, he lived in St. John, New Brunswick, working as an insurance salesman. He returned to Montreal a few years later, and started a men's clothing business with a partner. But they went bankrupt around 1930. So, he got a job with the Premier Brand Clothing Company, travelling to small towns in western Quebec and Ontario selling men's clothing.

Then he met Chaim Korenberg, father of Clara Korenberg, his wife-to-be.

"Clara was pushed into the marriage," David says. His tone turns bitter. "I think her father wanted to go into business with Abe. I don't know." He hands me the wedding invitation, dated January 17, 1932.

"Did they love each other?" I ask.

He shrugs. "Love didn't enter into it in those days."

We look at the wedding photos, large black and white prints of the bride and groom in classic poses. Young Clara holds a bouquet of roses, her head slightly tilted, looking to the side of the camera with a closed mouth, half a smile. To me it's a classic wedding pose, but David corrects me. "She was not a happy bride."

And that's when he reveals a piece of information which seems to belong to someone else's family.

"You see, my mother wanted to be a concert pianist. She even attended the McGill Conservatory for a year."

I look up at him. "Really?"

He nods, staring at the photo. "The piano your mother and I grew up with—it was Clara's. Years later I met one of her friends, a music teacher. She said Clara could have been one of the greats."

I think of the piano that I played as a child. I had known it was my mother's, but I hadn't realized it had come from her mother.

"What happened?"

"Her father pulled her out. Said he needed the money to educate *the boys*." He emphasizes the last two words with sarcasm, almost disdain. "Her life ended there."

I am still trying to absorb this information when he says, "But you want to know about my father." He puts the photo aside and goes back to the chronology of my grandfather.

All week, this new information about my grandmother nags at me, like a puzzle piece in search of a puzzle. I question my sisters and my father. It's news to them, too. I begin to have doubts. I decide to call Lela.

Lela is my late mother's cousin in Toronto. Lela's father, Morton Korenberg, was one of Clara's three brothers—"the boys" her father needed the money for.

I don't actually remember Lela. The last time I saw her was when I was ten, at my mother's funeral. Will she remember me?

I take a deep breath and pick up the phone.

Of course she remembers me. And she is delighted to tell me about her Aunt Clara.

Clara Korenberg was twelve years younger than Abe. Her parents too had fled the pogroms, leaving Kishenev, Russia (Bessarabia province) in 1905. She was born in Montreal, in 1909. Unlike Abe, she attended high school, graduating from Baron Byng in 1926.

"David said she wanted to be a pianist," I say.

"Oh yes, she was very talented," Lela says. "When her father pulled her out of the Conservatory, Mort was furious! She had a gift. As a musician himself, he could appreciate it."

Lela tells me the whole Korenberg family was musical. Once again I feel like I'm hearing about someone else's family—not my own great-uncles.

Morton was a prominent doctor at Montreal's Jewish General Hospital and later a psychiatrist. But originally, he almost studied music and composition. He had perfect pitch, sang, and played the piano and the violin.

Lela doesn't think Clara's father was trying to be cruel. "That's just the way women were treated. They got married and had children. Men earned a living to support the family. What did a woman need to go study music for?"

My parents read my early stories with enthusiasm. When I was in elementary school, my father brought home an old Ditto machine and I printed my own newspaper. But by university, I sensed that he wanted me to choose a "real" career, not some artsy English literature and journalism program. My sisters had chosen solid professions: architecture and computer science. "I only want you to be happy," my father would say—meaning, financially secure.

After graduating, I worked at a weekly paper. Occasionally I wrote short stories and sent them off to literary journals. Rejection letters followed. I went to Spain for a year, and found work as a translator. When I returned to Montreal and decided to study translation formally, my father seemed relieved. But my uncle said, "What happened to the writing?"

I decide to ask David more about Clara. We're sitting outside on his back patio, admiring a small grove of birch trees that separate his house from the neighbour's.

His parents had a hard life. As a travelling salesman, his father was away a lot. That was hard on Clara, who was left to manage on her own, without much money, raising two kids in their dark, second-floor apartment on Hutchison Street.

Clara's mother had died young. "My mother never learned how to cope," David says. As she grew older, Clara became bitter and paranoid. She thought her husband's family hated her. She kept more and more to herself. She grew suspicious of her husband when he was on the road. They fought. "Your mother blamed her for causing all these problems," David tells me. "I was the peacemaker, the glue holding the family together."

I ask David if he ever heard Clara play. No. She refused. It was a part of her life she couldn't have, so she wanted nothing more to do with it. But she encouraged her children to take lessons. Sally, my mother, did, but David didn't want to. He said it was "for girls." He regrets that now.

He does remember, once or twice, his mother showing Sally how to do something on the piano. His eyes take on a faraway look. "She didn't touch the piano—she caressed it." Whereas Sally banged away, Clara's touch was "magic, like an angel." He makes a delicate movement with his own hand, curving his wrist, remembering.

And he remembers the piano. His face becomes animated.

"I couldn't play, but I could put in a scroll and pump the pedals and watch it play," he says, laughing. He takes off his glasses to wipe them. "You know, it could probably still be restored—" he says, and I realize with dread … he doesn't know.

"We don't have it anymore," I say.

He pauses in cleaning his glasses. It's a fraction of a second but I catch a glimpse of something in those blue eyes. Maybe it's my imagination, but something changes in his face, like a smile fading, like a last piece of his mother's dream dying. I rush to explain how I had wanted to keep it, but it wasn't possible. Of course not, he says. He shakes his head and puts his glasses back on.

Driving home, it hits me. Why, ever since I was little, my uncle has always made a point of encouraging me in my writing, in my own artistic pursuits. His mother never had the chance to develop her talents, but I do.

I call Lela back. I don't really expect her to remember the piano, but she does.

"When I was small, we would go to Clara's house, and she would play it for us," she says.

"You heard her play?" I ask, surprised.

"Yes. She was very good."

I ask if she knows where the piano came from. She says that Clara's father bought it for her. I mention that I grew up with that piano, but that—

"You still have it?"

I can hear the hope in her voice. Once again, I have to break the news.

"Oh God, it was sold!" Her dismay and disappointment are palpable even over the phone. "It was so precious. Everyone played it."

I hardly remember my grandmother. I was nine years old when she died of cancer. I remember she wore square glasses, looked a lot like my mother, and was always shaking. Nervous. But nice to me.

I phone my step-mom to ask what became of the piano. She says they sold it to a young man from British Columbia who was studying at McGill University. They ran into him two years later in Pointe-Claire. He had moved and left it with a friend.

"I wish I could track it down," I say.

And she asks, "What would you do if you found it?"

I look down at the paper I've been doodling on while talking to her. Rows of triangles. I start to fill one in with my pen.

"I'm not sure," I say.

I send out a few messages on Facebook anyway, to look for it.

More importantly, I start to write my grandmother's story.

Staying Aloft

"I USED TO LOVE THIS," I say, pulling a dusty Tonka truck down from the shelf.

"Take it," my father urges. He rubs absently at the red sore in the middle of his brow.

"Why? What am I going to do with it?"

He shrugs. He digs in his pocket for a cigarette and concentrates on keeping his hand steady enough to light it.

I weigh the metal toy in my hands. I pull one of the levers and the miniature backhoe extends. Another lever flips the shovel. Wow. After all these years, it still works.

Yet another item to sort, as we choose what to keep and what to leave behind.

We're packing up the family country house in Vermont. My dad is selling it.

He and Hannah, my step-mom, used to spend at least three days a week here. It's where he flew his model airplanes. Flying in summer, repairing and building new ones in winter. Hannah would read, paint, write, knit blankets for her grandchildren. That was the routine.

But then my father's health started to deteriorate. As the years went by, they made the trip less and less often. The turning point came six months ago: the sudden debilitating pain, the operation, the incapacity.

It's just not doable anymore.

We lived in the city of Montreal, but every Friday night I'd climb into the backseat of the car between my two older sisters, and my parents would drive to the country house. Across the Champlain Bridge, past barns and hay silos and tractors and cows. The smell of fresh manure from fertilized fields permeated the car. We'd cross the border at Frelighsburg, wheels crunching on our gravel driveway about ten minutes later.

My father designed the house himself. He was an architect. He drew the plans and oversaw the workers as they poured concrete for the foundation, erected two-by-fours, hammered and sawed. He was a hands-on person. Over the years he built a shed, then a front extension, and later a stand-alone garage.

I can still picture him measuring and marking the wood as it lies across the sawhorses, making clean cuts with a circular saw, hoisting up walls, hammering them in place. I can smell the sawdust, which blankets the ground in a thin layer like a first snowfall.

Now, almost thirty years later, I wander the grounds. My childhood plays out before me, like in those movies where a character stands in an empty room and their past self materializes like a ghost.

I remember the cool dampness of summer nights, the lawn wet with dew, blades of grass sticking to my bare feet. Waiting each year for the fireflies to come out. One night I'd spot a flash, then another, little flares in the darkness. The following night there'd be more, flicking on and off against the dark shapes of the bushes. There's nothing more magical than fireflies.

The city meant school, friends, the daily routine. The country meant not just weekends but entire summers, sunburnt shoulders, swimming in the nearby lake, exploring tall grasses and forest, climbing the hill. Wading into brambles to pick wild blackberries, their sour-sweet juice filling my mouth.

I had all my favourite spots: behind the house, the grass slopes down to a majestic maple tree that burns red in the fall in the setting sun. Behind the tree runs a hedge of rocks, and beyond that lies an overgrown meadow populated by young trees, shrubs, tall grass and what my dad called "brush"—bushes of scratchy twigs with tiny leaves. Among these was my pine tree.

I'd duck under its branches and emerge inside a small "room," a protective space enclosed by the green-needled bows and surrounding bushes. It was just big enough for me to sit with a book or a snack. The ground was soft and spongey from the layers of dried pine needles, some sticky with fragrant sap. Peering between the branches, I was hidden but could still see the house. A perfect spot for spying.

I liked sitting there. It was a private place where I could be alone with my thoughts, listen to bird calls, hug my knees and sort out complicated or uncomfortable feelings.

The first time I brought Michael, my fiancé, to the country house, I led him into the garage to see the model airplanes. There were more than I'd remembered. Some had wingspans of up to six feet. The colours were bold: yellow and red, white and blue, often with a stripe or decal on the wing ("so that you can tell if it's right-side up when it's in the air," my dad once explained). Close up they looked like giant cartoon bugs, with cockpit eyes and a big engine nose, and propeller blades for whiskers. Giant bugs sitting on worktables, hanging from the ceiling, stacked on a rack. Michael took dozens of pictures with his digital camera.

My father built a runway for his planes—a strip of grass about fifty feet wide and fifty yards long, running parallel to the road. Every spring when the ground had thawed, he'd flatten the bumps as best he could with a roller, a big water-filled drum with a handle like a lawn mower, and every week in the summer the grass had to be cut short. For a while the task fell to my two older sisters, each pushing a mower up and down in the hot sun, until my father bought a motor-powered one that you could sit on. He loved to drive it himself, in a pattern of tighter and tighter circles, like a Zamboni.

When I was little, my mom made me stay inside while my father flew his planes—"just in case." When I got a bit older, I would stand at the edge of the runway with my sisters and watch.

Our job was to follow the plane with our eyes so we could help him find it if it crashed. Crashes were exciting. We'd hear the sudden crunch of the plane hitting a tree and then abrupt silence when the whine of the motor cut—or the motor would cut first and then there'd be a few seconds of suspense, followed by a thump. My sisters and I would dash through the tall grass and bushes, ignoring scratches to our bare legs and arms as we raced to be first to the scene. My father followed in more measured strides. Sometimes it took a few minutes to dislodge the plane from the branches. Then he'd hold it up at arm's length, assessing the damage, and carry it back to his workshop with us nipping at his heels.

Winter was for repairing the planes, making improvements, or building new ones. My father spent countless hours in his basement workshop, cigarette hanging off his lip, measuring, sketching, cutting, sanding, gluing. There was always some airplane part lying on sheets of newspaper on the ping-pong table. A tubular body, shiny with fresh paint. The skeleton of a wing, waiting to be wrapped in thin fabric. Whenever I came inside from playing in the snow and descended the unfinished wood stairs to the basement, my nostrils filled with the smells of cigarette smoke, airplane glue and solvent.

I was never close with my father. Neither before nor after my mother's death. We were not a family that got "close."

Once, when I was six or seven years old, I went to the country house alone with him. I don't remember why my mother and sisters weren't there, only that it felt like a treat. My father was always around, but he wasn't really involved in my life. So spending a whole weekend, just me and him, was exciting. I wasn't sure what to expect.

He made scrambled eggs. And that is all I remember. I guess it stuck in my mind because, at that time, my father didn't cook. Except for French toast—that was his specialty—and grilling hotdogs and steaks on the barbecue. His steaks tended to be burnt on the outside and raw inside. We teased him about that; it was a family joke. So maybe he cooked steaks that night and I don't remember because it wasn't unusual. But him frying eggs, just for the two of us, that was a novelty. They looked different from the ones my mom cooked, with black specs that may have been pepper or may have been burnt leftovers from the pan. They tasted different too, although I can't say in what way.

After a morning of packing, we go into Enosburg Falls and pull up at the gas station. Hannah chats with the attendant, a boy of about nineteen, who also clears their driveway in winter and does odd jobs around the house. They discuss the weather. He inquires about my dad's health. In the parking lot next door, a woman with two children in tow slides shuts a minivan door before heading into the big Brooks pharmacy. It used to be the Grand Union, the town's main grocery store, before the giant Hannaford's was built. That was also before there was a McDonald's. And again, I see ghosts, my sisters and I piling out of the car.

"Can we get ice cream? Or a watermelon? Can we get a watermelon?"

"We'll get ice cream *and* a watermelon," my mother says, as we enter the cool air of the grocery store.

On rainy days, we'd drive to a hobby shop near Burlington. I'd wander up and down the aisles of the crafts section looking at Styrofoam balls and wicker baskets while my dad would stand at the counter with the salesman, pulling an airplane engine from a box and debating its merits. Or we'd go to the hardware store, where my mind would go numb from staring at endless rows of wrenches while my father peered into little drawers of screws, one after another, absorbed in the minutiae and comfort of mechanical objects.

My father sits on a drafting stool in the basement, smoking. His left hand shakes; the tremor is a symptom of his disease. In the middle of his furrowed brow, a red welt glistens. The sore appears when he is stressed. I suspect it first developed when my mother was sick, reaching its worst when she died. Then faded away after he met Hannah. Now it's back. Frustrated and angry.

My father surveys the worktables covered in tools, the shelves lined with labelled cigar boxes where he keeps spare parts, the jars of screws and cans of nails. He has already packed up boxes of model airplane engines, his pocket knife collection, tools for my sister, tools for me, and still, every tool imaginable can be found down here in this basement: Exacto knives, screwdrivers of all sizes, pliers, wrench sets, awls, sanding blocks, clamps, scales, heat guns, drills, wires, chains, scrapers, hammers, magnifying glasses, pocket flashlights, rubber bands, Ziplock bags, cleaning cloths, glues, solvents, saws, planes, rulers, padlocks and keys, bolts, nuts, hooks, goggles, levels, tape measures, and hundreds of objects whose name and purpose elude me. Every drawer of every cabinet reveals more.

He puffs at his cigarette and surveys his domain. Thirty years of collecting, building and "puttering"—his favourite expression—have come to a standstill. He'll sell the house with most of its contents. He goes through drawers trying to decide what to salvage; one last look, just one more item.

About six years ago, the doctors confirmed that my father's "bum leg" was Parkinson's. The symptoms grew more pronounced. One night I watched him cook dinner and was startled by how the spatula shook in his hand as he spooned fish onto the plates. With a cocktail of pills, he was still going about his usual routine. Until this year. Suddenly, he developed a crippling pain in his back and in his good leg. In the space of six months, he went from leading an independent life of work and travel to needing someone to help him dress. An operation to create space around the spinal nerves and between the discs relieved some of the pain, but it did not restore his mobility. He can't walk far, or sit for too long, or bend, or twist.

I hear Hannah upstairs, shuffling through papers and books. The floor creaks with indecision.

Michael and I are in the garage. More tools, a collection of antique cameras, shelves of R/C Modeler magazines, an Underwood typewriter, an antique dresser, and some of my old toys. I point to the metal Tonka truck that I found earlier.

"My father gave that to me after my eye operation," I say.

"Really? Why don't you keep it?" Michael asks.

I was four years old. The operation was meant to correct my lazy eye, which was so bad that sometimes I saw double.

In the first few days of my recovery, I'd wake up with lids glued shut. My mother would apply cotton balls and warm water to coax them open. One morning I opened my gummy eyes to a big box wrapped up like a birthday gift. Inside was this fantastic truck. I spent hours playing with it, digging and shovelling. My sandbox transformed into a construction site.

Another father might have bought his daughter a doll. But that's just how my father was: ever the practical, mechanical mind. I can just picture him at the toy store. He'd have gone to the counter and taken it out of the box to examine it, just like he did with the model airplane engines. He'd have chosen a brand name product, the slightly more expensive model, not because he liked flashy things but for its guarantee of reliability and durability.

I must have been nine when my mother was diagnosed with breast cancer. Most of my memories of her illness take place in the city, not the country. Except for two: in the first memory, my mother sits on the patio behind the house, enjoying the sun. She isn't wearing her wig. A friend comes by, unannounced, and catches sight of my mother's bald head. She is mortified. Her friend says it's okay. Then they both laugh. I am astonished. Caught off-guard myself.

In the second memory, my dad and my mother are fighting. Shouting. My dad is furious. I'm terrified he's going to hit her; she is so weak. He slams our wood salad bowl to the floor. It cracks in two. Our beautiful wood salad bowl. My sister Anne pulls me away, out of the house, up the hill to one of the spots we always go. I am crying. Anne is telling me he isn't going to hurt Mom, don't worry. Five years my senior, maybe she understood that he, too, was terrified.

My father loved my mother. I remember mornings when I'd come in to their room to wake them or crawl into their bed for a hug, and they'd be holding each other. I remember his red eyes the day I came home from school and he told me that she'd died.

I don't remember what it was like at the country house the first year after her death. I imagine that we went, and that my dad still flew his planes, and that my oldest sister Lisa shared the cooking. But it's a blur.

I stopped going to the country house at some point in my teens, when I was finally old enough to stay home alone with my sisters and hang out with my friends in the city. Later, as a young adult, I'd visit now and then—a stopover on my way to a cross-country ski lodge, or on my way back from a hiking trip. I'd check on my old haunts—under the pine tree, along the creek, up the hill. They were overgrown and hard to find, but still there. Meanwhile, my dad had remarried. He and Hannah had a whole life in the country, with their own hobbies, friends and activities. Each time I visited there was some addition—a new ride-on mower, a second shed, the garage.

At thirty-two, I met Michael, my soulmate and future husband. One day, we decided to go to the country house alone, when my parents were not there. We planned a weekend getaway. And then, only then, did I finally understand why people have country houses. Trees whispering in the wind, soft grass, the sweet scent of clover, grasshoppers flitting about, birds calling to each other, crickets chirping, the absence of traffic. Rest. Peace. I felt like I could stay all week, reading and writing, going for walks, sipping wine and staring at the stars.

I realized, too, how lucky I'd been to grow up in this place. The important part it had played in shaping my view of the world and who I was. I imagined bringing my own kids here one day.

Then my father announced his plans to sell.

The ground under my feet started to crumble. Incredulous, I struggled to regain my balance.

Sell the house he built with his own two hands, his home away from home, his refuge? Sell the homestead that was both workshop and operating base for his radio-controlled model airplanes, his cherished and lifelong passion?

But that was the crux of the matter. He hadn't flown his planes for years. Hadn't tinkered with them, or puttered. His eyesight was going, and Parkinson's had robbed him of fine motor control.

And now, for the past six months, the debilitating back pain confined him to specific chairs and walks of no more than thirty feet.

At first, I thought about offering to take over. I couldn't afford the upkeep, but I could put in the labour. Go down once a month. I mulled it over, thinking there was time. But my family doesn't talk. At least, my father and I don't. By the next time we spoke, he'd already shaken hands over a deal. And riding back with my parents the following Saturday, crossing the United States–Canada border, sitting in traffic, I realized that I could not commit to this anyway. I had a life to live in the city, my own house to buy, maybe even a baby within the next few years.

Coming down each month would be a chore, not a pleasure. It would be years until my future children would be old enough to enjoy it, to explore the land on their own, to roam its hills, forests and fields and embark on self-made adventures, the way I had done growing up. I might not even be living in Montreal anymore.

Best to let go. I'd start fresh with my own family, rent places in the summer, go camping. Create my own traditions.

"It must be hard to see your father reduced to this," my father said to me once, when I visited him at the hospital. He'd lost thirty pounds since the operation and could barely turn over in bed. The room was a dull green, impersonal, and smelled of disinfectant.

"You're still the same Dad to me," I said, shrugging. I meant it. He was still Dad: sharp, knowledgeable and obstinate. The patriarch. Worrying about everything and disapproving of all my life choices— except for getting engaged to Michael.

What makes the illness so hard is that our family dynamic isn't set up for this. We don't talk about what we really think or feel. Emotions are uncomfortable. How do you cope with disease and decline when feelings are taboo? I am an adult now. I can no longer hide under the branches of a pine tree.

On one of our packing missions, Hannah comes across a videotape of Dad flying his airplanes. It was filmed about ten years earlier. We slide it into the VCR.

There's Dad, walking down the grass runway, holding the radio transmitter out in front of him with both hands, thumbs on the control levers, antenna forward. The airplane bobs along the grass ahead of him like a puppy. Its propeller is a blur. The engine screams like a high-pitched weed-cutter, slowing as my dad drives it to the end of the runway and turns it around. Then, standing still, he sends it back down the runway on its own. The plane gathers speed, the pitch of the motor rising, and then the nose lifts and the pitch changes again as the plane breaks free of the ground and soars into the air.

Here the camera has difficulty following the plane as it weaves in and out of view, circling overhead, then across the fields and back.

My dad shows off with a loop-de-loop, turning the plane upside-down. Somewhat abruptly, the film cuts to the landing, the plane flying in low and then touching down, bobbing over the grass and then coming to a standstill. The video cuts again to my father wiping down the plane with a cloth.

Watching this, I can smell the fuel lingering around the plane's hot engine. I see, too, the ghost of the wooden box he'd carry out with the plane when he was getting ready to fly. It smelled of grease and freshly cut grass. He'd set it on the ground, open the front panel and pull out little tubes of lubricant and starter fluid. He'd use the remote control to check the servos, wiggling the wing and tail flaps. Then he'd start the engine. In the early days this meant flicking the propeller around with his finger until the engine caught. In later years, he used a device that inserted into the centre of the propeller. Then he'd turn the plane around by the tail, straighten, and walk it out to the end of the runway.

One thing, though: my father never let other people fly his planes. Not my mom, not me, not my sisters. Sometimes I'd bring a friend to the country house for the weekend, and they'd ask for a turn. They didn't understand: these planes were not toys. They were my father's heart and soul.

He did let my middle sister fly one, once. Then started yelling at her because she was doing it all wrong (in his mind). I don't remember what happened. I think he grabbed the controller out of her hands and she started crying. I just know that it did not end well.

He was never good at giving up control.

Driving home one Saturday, my father says, "Who am I kidding? I'm taking home all these tools as if I'm going to start building model airplanes again."

"So what if you don't?" Hannah says. "There are other things to do in life."

"I suppose," my father says.

He does not sound convinced.

I never tired of watching the planes. Why is that? Why is it mesmerizing to follow a contraption whizzing through the air, the familiar whine rising and falling in pitch in accordance with the doppler effect, while your own heart beats fast? As if some primordial part of you is still astonished at the ability of an object other than a bird to stay aloft.

The next time back, the realization hits me like a blast of winter air let into a warm cozy room: we are selling the house. I won't see it anymore. I won't be able to say on a whim, "Hey, let's go to Vermont for the weekend!" and arrive to see the same building, unchanged, and let myself in to find the same books on the shelves, the same coats on the rack, and the same kitchen pots on their pegs.

But it is not so much the loss of the house that bothers me.

It is the loss of this place.

On the drive home that night, grief engulfs me. My limbs feel heavy, like they are being held underwater. My throat is tight. Clouds seep across the sky, darkening my vision.

I think of my sisters, both living far away. They don't have to go through any of this. Out of sight, out of mind. No favourite spots or objects to trigger memories.

Then again, perhaps it would not have been the same for them at all. They both have their own families and homes now. They've already begun creating their own traditions.

I don't pause to consider how hard it must be for my father to let go.

It's our last visit.

I stand on the gravel driveway, breathing in the air one last time. Green and fresh. Earthy.

A hint of creosote emanates from the planks of the house heating in the sun.

I close my eyes. I can feel the pebbles under my running shoes shift and then settle. A breeze brushes my arms. I listen to the trees swaying and rustling in its wake, rising and falling in waves. Voices from a nearby farm echo in the distance.

My father and Hannah are still inside—they have a friend helping with the final chores.

My dad will be meeting his lawyer next week to sign the papers.

So, this is it.

I open my eyes.

On impulse, I dart back into the garage.

The workbenches are bare. The airplanes are gone. Some have been packed away for storage in Montreal. Others have been sold or given away. The tractor-mower and snow blower are parked along one wall, ready for the next owner. But I am looking for something else. It's sitting on a shelf beside a lone badminton racket and a coffee can filled with nails.

The Tonka truck.

I take it down and examine it. It's heavy, none of this light, cheap moulded plastic most toys are made of today. Some of the metal has rusted. Once again, I see my father oiling the joints and testing the levers, with the same care he applied to checking the wheels on his airplanes or the movement of the wing flaps. A bit of dirt still clings to one of the tires.

And then I am in the sandbox again, sun beating down on the back of my neck, insects buzzing in the tall grass beside me.

I toss the truck onto the backseat of the car. I take my place behind the wheel and begin the drive home.

The hum of an airplane fades into the distance.

PART III
NEW VOICES

Tiny Fists

FAR AWAY, a voice pulls me from the depths of sleep.

"Mrs. Krakow to the nursery, please."

Has it been three hours already? The hospital bed creaks as I struggle to push myself up to the intercom. "Coming, thank you."

Michael, my husband, is already up from his cot, pulling on his sweatpants. We step out into the bright, neon-lit hallway and make our way gingerly, dragging my IV pole along. My bottom aches. I'm shivering.

We arrive at the intensive care nursery, or ICN. We wash our hands with antibacterial soap. My skin itches from the constant washing. We don clean blue hospital robes and make our way over to our baby, where the nurse has turned off the incubator's ultraviolet lights and is unhooking the IV from the back of his tiny hand. His eyes are still closed and his face twists into a whine; he just wants to sleep. I sit on a chair with a pillow in my lap. The nurse places little Alex in my arms. His body is warm against my skin. I stop shivering.

He is so small, so fragile, that I am afraid to move. He fits into my two hands. His body is reddish, and there are strawberry patches on his eyelids. His nose and cheeks are tinged yellow from jaundice. Blond fuzz covers his body. He still has splotches of dried blood on his hands and face, and there's a big scab on his head from scraping on my pelvic bone. I'd skimmed the chapter in my prenatal book about preemies. It had warned of a scrawny appearance, wrinkles, translucent skin, no nipples, poor muscle tone. But Alex looks perfect to me. In fact, later, when I catch a glimpse of a full-term newborn, I find it big and ugly, like a cabbage-patch doll.

Michael pulls a folding screen around us, and we begin the routine. I am trying to get Alex to breastfeed, but he won't latch on. The nurse says it's because he's premature. "Keep trying," she says. But Alex keeps falling asleep. "Tickle his toes." Soon he gets frustrated and begins to cry. So I hand him over to Michael, who feeds him from a medicine cup—Alex laps it up like a kitten—while I go "pump."

"Twenty minutes on each breast," the nurse said the very first day, showing me how to operate the breast pump, a plastic-encased machine with dials for speed and intensity. "Every three hours," she added, "or your milk will dry up." I fit on my personal attachment, hold the silicon cup onto my breast and turn a dial. The machine begins chugging, and the cup suctions onto my skin. My whole nipple is sucked in and out, as if you'd stuck a vacuum cleaner onto my chest. The pressure is uncomfortable at first, but it doesn't hurt.

I attach a bottle to the tube at the other end, and at first it sucks dry, just a few drops of colostrum, a sticky yellow fluid that the nurse collects with a dropper as if it were God's own honey. After a day or two it's more of a milky yellow, and then my milk "comes in." I produce bottles of rich, thick milk, and the nurses commend me on my quality milk supply. I am a prize-winning cow.

Every three hours. During the day I wheel one of the breast pumps available at the nursing station over to my hospital bed. But at night I don't want to wake the others in the ward, so I stay in the little room at the back of the ICN. They try to make it comfy, with padded chairs and screens with hearts and Care Bears, but the older, industrial-looking machines look like torture devices.

Because Alex was born five weeks early, weighing just five-pounds-nine-ounces, we are to feed him every three hours, around the clock. Subtract the time of the feeding itself and my pumping, and I barely get two hours to sleep. And I need to eat, too. After a few days we give in to the nurses' suggestion to let them do one of the night feedings. But I still have to get up to pump. My breasts get so full they become hard and painful and begin to leak, and I wake up, the front of my shirt soaked.

A friend comes to visit and I am embarrassed. It's not really an IV on the pole that I'm dragging around. At the bottom of the pole hangs a bag collecting my urine. I haven't been able to pee since Alex was born.

Friends were visiting that first day too, and I actually felt good after a shower, still buoyed by the drugs. But by four o'clock, the pressure in my bladder was so strong that it felt like it would burst, and I was scared. I sat with a forced smile and willed my friends to leave. I had to see the nurse. Immediately.

She had me lie on the bed and inserted a Foley catheter, reassuring me. "It happens sometimes." She removed the catheter after twenty-four hours, but still, nothing would come out. A different nurse inserted the next one (this time it was excruciating as she routed around my swollen private parts) and said to wait another forty-eight hours. The catheter pinches now and then, but otherwise it just adds to the general soreness of my swollen bottom. I can't feel my urine coming out but I see the bag fill. I'm supposed to call the nurse whenever it needs to be emptied.

Every three hours. The lights are always on at the ICN. Daytime is busy with visitors, but at night, the only people allowed in are breast-feeding mothers and their partners. There's a subdued quiet, punctuated by the occasional crying baby or monitor beeping.

A different nurse is on duty and sees us cup-feeding.

"He's not getting enough like that," she says, alarmed. "You have to bottle-feed him."

"We were told the bottle will confuse him if we're trying to breast-feed," I say.

"Doesn't matter. He needs to eat."

Why didn't anyone tell us sooner?

They've removed the catheter but I still can't pee. I've tried warm showers and running water but it's just not working. Another nurse inserts a catheter for the third time, and I demand to see a urologist. Tomorrow, I'm told.

Alex still isn't latching on. The nurses try to help us when they can but they're often busy tending to other babies. He isn't gaining enough weight, either.

My world is the fourth floor of the hospital. It is the chugging of the breast pump, the pressure on my breast as it sucks the milk out of me. It is the shy smiles exchanged with other struggling couples in the ICN. It is cold food waiting for me on a tray when I return from feeding my baby. Every three hours.

All I want to do is cuddle my newborn. But the only contact we have is the frustrating experience of trying to feed. Maybe the nurses would let me just sit there and hold him, I don't know. But I have to pump. I have to sleep. I have to eat. I want to snatch Alex away and shut out the world.

In our prenatal class, we'd watched a video of a woman using an electric breast pump. She was pumping both breasts at once; she looked like a cow in a milking barn. The guy sitting beside me had laughed. I remember thinking, *I can't picture myself ever doing that.*

Right now I'd like to find the guy who laughed and punch him in the face.

I'm sitting on my bed pumping when a passing nurse sees me.

"You shouldn't keep pumping once the milk stops flowing," she says.

But I was told twenty minutes on each side! My throat aches from trying not to cry.

Upon my insistence Michael has left the room to get himself some food, when the urologist appears. He prods my stomach for about a minute and then declares he'll leave the catheter in and send me home with a leg bag. A nurse from my community health clinic will come remove it next week. The urologist picks up his clipboard and shrugs his shoulders. "It happens sometimes," he says. "Not often, but it happens."

But there's one problem: a test showed I have a bladder infection, so I'll have to take antibiotics. The nurse explains what this means: I won't be able to breastfeed. If I want to continue afterward, then I'll have to keep pumping while on the antibiotics, so that my milk doesn't dry up. But I'll have to throw the milk away.

The tears rush forth.

I try to speak but I can't. I sit there on the edge of the hospital bed sobbing, my vision blurring from tears, the nurse holding my hand and trying to say comforting things.

They say a mother will do anything for her child. I picture myself pumping every three hours for seven days, and pouring the milk down the sink. I am crying because I don't think I can do it. I am crying because I probably will.

In the end, I am spared. The doctor finds an antibiotic that I can take while still breastfeeding. And so the routine continues.

Alex is out of the incubator, in a clear plastic bassinet. We coo to him as we unwrap the layers of cotton sheets, and as he cranes his neck and yawns and stretches his little arms and legs, I say, "Stretchy, stretch!" And smile. He opens his big blue eyes.

I suddenly remember something the nurse said right after Alex was born. I'd had a very long and exhausting pushing phase—four hours—because his head had been at a weird angle. She said I had been "very brave." But bravery had nothing to do with it—what choice did I have? Perhaps that was my first taste of what it means to be a mother. I caress his downy blond head and watch him drink from his bottle, tiny fists curled under his chin.

The next day, I am discharged. I step outside and breathe fresh air for the first time in seven days. When I entered the hospital it was fall, but now there is snow and slush on the ground, and it is cold. The world has changed to winter.

It feels amazing to sleep in my own bed but the night is short—we cannot bear to be away from our baby. For three days we shuttle back and forth, trying to sleep on chairs in the cafeteria or the waiting room in between feedings. At one point, we watch the couple next to us dressing their baby in layers and fitting her into a car seat. When will they let us bring our baby home? We keep asking to speak to the pediatrician, but he works at three hospitals and seems to only visit ours when we're not there.

Then, on day ten, the nurses give us the message: Alex is free to go.

We are all home. We are all home, home, home at last. Our baby is asleep, wrapped like a burrito in his receiving blanket, a blue dot in his big crib. The apartment is so quiet.

As the hours pass, Michael begins to pace. He peeks into the crib whenever Alex stirs. He peeks in whenever Alex gets too quiet. Finally he looks at me and blurts out, "How are we going to manage without a room full of professional caregivers? How will he ever survive?"

He calls his best friend, who has two kids, for reassurance.

I sit on the couch, calm, pumping.

Under Construction

I YELL AND SLAM the bathroom door. Seconds later I regret the action. From within, my daughter lets out a protest scream. Short and sharp.

Some mother I am, exploding at my four-year-old over tooth brushing.

It's not that Aviva refuses to brush her teeth. It's all her little conditions that have to be met, one after another, everything just so. First she wants Dada, then Mama, then she wants to brush herself, then she wants me to brush, so I start to, but then she pushes my hand away and says she wants the stool so she can see in the mirror, you don't need to see in the mirror if Mama is brushing, want stool, well the stool is in the kitchen so go get it quickly, no Mama get it, no you're big enough to get it yourself, no you, let's just brush your teeth without it then, no, want to see in mirror—every morning and every night until the pressure builds and builds inside my whole body, ready to explode.

Slam.

Scream.

At age forty-two, I'm not exactly a young mother. I used to tell people this was not a bad thing. It meant I was more mature, more relaxed, because I could see the bigger picture. Lately, though, I'm not so sure. I worry too much, try to control too much, run out of patience too fast.

I close my eyes. Breathe. Did my mother yell at me? If I can't remember, then the answer must be no. Wait, once. I was about Aviva's age. I don't remember what I'd done, only that my mother was mad at me. My mother, standing a few feet in front of me but seeming worlds away, her tone harsh, her eyes angry. Me, crying. All I wanted was for her to hold me, love me. I moved toward her and at first she pushed me away, voice firm. But a moment later her voice softened, her angry features melted, and she gathered me back into her arms. I buried myself in the folds of her clothes. Reassured. I was where I needed to be.

A faint *"whack"* of plastic hitting wood comes from the bathroom, slightly muted by the closed door. I suspect my daughter has just hurled her toothbrush at it.

Before I had kids, I had all these ideas of what I would and wouldn't do. *I won't spoil my children. My child won't have a tantrum in the middle of the grocery store.* I remember visiting my cousin when I was pregnant with my first child. After dinner, my cousin excused herself to go lie down with her four-year-old to get him to sleep. *I won't be doing that when my kid is four*, I thought. *She'll learn to sleep on her own.*

So guess who lies down with her four-year-old every night. I'll even defend it by saying that Aviva falls asleep really quickly anyway, so what's the harm? And it's a great chance to relax and cuddle, and how much longer will I be able to do that? "They grow up so fast" isn't just an expression. My kids truly are different people today than they were two months ago.

I had lots of other notions about raising kids. *I'll set limits. I'll stay calm. I won't give in.* I was an "A" student at school, but in motherhood I'm pretty much a fail.

"Mama!" my daughter yells from the other side of the door. She's crying. I go in and pick her up. Aviva clings like a koala bear and buries her face in my neck. "Mama."

As I watch my children, I wonder what childhood memories are being created. What images, what seemingly meaningless incidents are going to stay with them, stick in their minds, their muscles, their skin?

Aviva and her seven-year-old brother Alex are dancing in the basement. They jump from sofa to carpet, hopping and gyrating their hips in a way I learned only as an adult. They crease their brows and declaim emphatically into imaginary microphones. Aviva comes over to where I'm sitting and takes my head in her two little hands, puts her face right up to mine so that our foreheads touch, grins with silliness and kisses me on both cheeks, then on the forehead. Tiny moist lips pecking my flesh. Then she giggles and goes back to dancing.

She is so alert, so aware, so sure.

When Alex was a baby, he'd squirm and complain so much in his crib that my husband and I would end up putting him on the bed in between us, next to our heads. Once, I woke up in the middle of the night and turned my head, and there was Alex, lying awake, staring at me with his large eyes. For a moment, I wondered if he could see in the dark like a cat. What nature of creature was he?

Even now, perhaps even more so, it seems inconceivable that my husband and I created these two beings.

I grab my son roughly by the shoulders and steer him down the hall. "Ow!" he yells. I thrust him into his room.

"You stay here until you're ready to talk nicely," I shout, slamming his door shut.

"I hate you! I'm never talking to you again!" he screams.

I am shaking with anger and shame. I've done it again. Lost my temper. No wonder he hits and screams and threatens to break his toys when he gets mad. I walk back to the kitchen, forcing myself to take slow steps.

My daughter is sitting at the table, unfazed, shoving noodles into her mouth with her fingers. "My brother's in a bad mood," Aviva says.

I feel completely drained.

I can't help thinking of my own mother. As I suspect countless generations of women have done since the dawn of time when they have become mothers themselves. How did she do it? Did she yell at my older sisters? Did she have endless patience and calm? Was she strict? Was I more pliable?

My mother is no longer alive to answer these questions.

I twirl my spaghetti around my fork and marvel at the perfect bundle it makes.

Once, at our family country house, I was playing in the field and gathered a bouquet for my mother. I must have been about Alex's age. It was August, hot, the trees busy with birdcalls, grasshoppers jumping up from the grass in front of my feet. I made a bouquet of what we called "brush," stuff that grew like weeds. The plants were dry at that time of year, and the ends had little burly clumps that, to me, looked like flowers.

I held them behind my back, beaming and proud, about to present them to my mother. I was already anticipating the smile that would bloom on her face.

"You didn't pick wild flowers, did you?" my mother said before I could show them to her. "You know you shouldn't pick wild flowers."

My face fell. Tears welled. I dropped the bouquet, turned and ran.

"Wait, it's okay!" my mother called after me. In my mind's eye, I see her stooping to pick up the dry twigs.

But it was too late.

How could she even *think* I would pick wild flowers? Of course, I knew not to pick wild flowers!

I ran until I knew I was out of sight and then cried and cried.

I'd brought a gift and was met with lack of trust and unwarranted reproach.

Now, when I make a mistake or say something that accidentally moves my son from buoyant happiness to tears of hurt, I wonder, years from now, is this a moment he will remember? Is it being etched in his mind, marking him, shaping him in ways that I did not intend?

I see a blue *Thomas the Tank Engine* blanket creeping slowly across the kitchen floor.

"Is that a blanket-boy?" I ask softly.

There is a muffled "*mreu*" sound.

"Come sit on your chair. I'll wrap the blanket around you."

Five minutes later Alex is happily eating and chattering away.

I listen but part of me has not caught up yet, pondering what scars are being left, what codes imprinted on my children's neuron-firing brains.

Aviva sits on my lap at the dinner table. She has finished her meal but I'm still eating. This is where Aviva loves to be: on Mommy's lap, in Mommy's arms. More than Alex. In some ways she is more independent, more social, less shy, but she always comes back to this place.

And suddenly I remember. Mornings when I'd come into the dining room after waking to find my mother sitting at the head of the oval teak table, reading the paper, holding a mug of tea. I'd climb up onto her lap. My mother would still be wearing her flannel dressing gown, and I'd nestle against her, enveloped in the fabric, in her scent, in that soft and warm space. That is what I remember. How warm it was, how safe I felt, how happy I was. It was the best place in the world.

Alex is in his room banging and throwing things. I told him he can't play Nintendo because it's a school night and now he's mad.

First it's the Lego. "I knew I would lose that piece, I knew it!" he yells.

Then he strips his bed: blanket, pillows, sheets. He pulls it all off. "Argh!" he screams.

I remain calm. In control. I speak in a normal voice. Firm and deliberate. I am proud of how calm I am managing to stay as he presses every button, hard.

"Why aren't you getting mad?" he finally shouts. "Why aren't you yelling?"

I stare at him in disbelief.

It's the middle of the night and I'm nudged awake by someone climbing into the bed. My eyes fight the darkness to figure out which child. Alex.

I raise myself onto an elbow to squint at the digital clock: 4:43 a.m. Should I take him back to his own bed?

He snuggles up to me under the covers, little hands curled up, knees pressing in, seeking warmth.

I settle back onto my pillow and put my arm around him. I inhale the scent of his hair. I kiss his forehead.

In the end, maybe this is all that matters. I may run out of patience, but I won't run out of love. Maybe as long as my children know this, they'll be okay.

I lie awake for a long time.

Little Tiger: Letter to My Daughter

WHEN YOU WERE LITTLE, I waited at the bottom of the slide, arms ready to catch you. Your sundress sliding down the warm plastic turned my touch into electric shocks. You looked at me in surprise and then laughed. Then one day I watched you climb the big-kid ladder after your brother. Limbs barely long enough to ford the gaps. Forced myself not to follow, not to hover. Let go. Let go.

Your middle name is Tiger after your grandmother's maiden name, but we changed "i" to "y." Tyger, tyger, burning bright. Strong and daring and bold. Your hair the scent of sun-drenched days, damp with sweet sweat, running and running, you never stop. Still my little kitten nestling up to me at night, purring, skin soft and warm. Who needs this more, me or you?

I made it to the top of the tree today, you announce with pride. My heart clenches. Sounds of branches cracking, thump on hard earth, broken bones, concussion. Breathe in. Bite tongue. *Today's urban youth suffer from nature deficit.* I tell you that's wonderful. My little kitten climbing up a tree.

Your room is a swirl of fruity lip balm and vanilla-scented candles. Your carpet a forest of Barbie dolls, Barbie clothes, Playmobil people, a yellow Fisher Price school bus, pony figurines, storybooks, adventure novels, papers, drawings, secret diaries, pencils and pens. Your wall a collage of the birthday cards I've made each year, hugs and cats and hearts.

Tigers are good swimmers. Their roars can be heard up to three kilometres away. Every tiger in the world is unique: no two tigers have the same pattern of stripes.

Can I go to my friend's house after school, you ask. Please, please, it's only six blocks. I don't say, look both ways before crossing the street. I don't say, beware of strangers. I don't say, stay on the path. I've said it before. Too many times. What will happen when you're older? Will your eyes turn fierce? Will you hide your heart? Never, you promise, your moist kisses on my cheek as binding as they are ephemeral.

Perennial

IT IS NIGHT. I lie next to my daughter on her bed. Our faces are so close that our noses almost touch. By the street light filtering through the curtains, I can make out her soft features.

"I love you," she whispers.

"I love you too," I whisper back.

"I love you more," she says.

"I love you even more," I say.

"But I love you most," she says.

"Impossible," I say. "It's impossible to love more than I love you."

It's a game we play, a litany we recite every night. She cannot know how true it is.

Later I say good night to my son. He curls under his blanket but holds my hand. He does not say anything. He is the quiet one. Like I was.

I was ten years old when my mother died. She was two years younger than I am now, a strange and frightening thought. But I no longer think in terms of my age. I think in terms of my children's ages. My son is eleven. My daughter is eight. In her eyes, her world is perfect. At her age, mine was too.

My mother never talked to me directly about love. I certainly felt loved, but our family never discussed it. We only talked about practical stuff.

A few years ago, when I was researching my family tree, my uncle told me something I hadn't heard before. "Your mother had only one regret," he said. "She wished she'd had more time with you." While she'd done all she could to prepare my two older sisters for life, she would have liked another three years with me.

I understand that now. Not just because I have my own children. But because it was only later in life that I truly began to feel her absence.

When my children were really little, I decided we should plant a vegetable garden. Living in a big city and buying everything at a grocery store, I felt it was important for them to know where food comes from. To have the experience of watching and nurturing something as it grows. I cleared a small patch at the side of the house, in the sun, and rented a car from the car-sharing service to lug two bags of dark earth home from the hardware store. I'm not a gardener, but I have a basic knowledge of what you're supposed to do.

When I was growing up, my mother had a huge vegetable garden at our country house. I can still see her, in her brown tank top and wide-brimmed hat, crouched among the rows of bean plants, pulling out weeds.

She'd spend the winter poring over catalogues, circling seed varieties and taking notes. She'd start the seedlings indoors—tomatoes, peppers, celery. My father built her a rack with special lights. As soon as it was dry enough in the spring, she'd get my father to plow the patch with the garden tiller. It got a little bigger each time. One year they had manure delivered, a big pile dumped at the top of the patch, and they used shovels to spread it over the earth before tilling. You got used to the smell when you spent enough time in the country.

I waited until my children were home from school and day care to spread the bags of earth. I knew they'd love plunging their hands into the soft, moist dirt. Aviva tried to lift the bag, which weighed as much as she did. Alex took tiny handfuls and carefully spread them on the patch.

I opened up a bag of carrot seeds. I didn't remember they'd be so tiny. I traced a line in the earth with my finger and instructed the kids to put the seeds in, not too close together. Aviva immediately dumped a whole pile in one spot. Alex shook some into his palm, but they were so tiny, he kept losing them. Next we tried lettuce; just as tiny, just as hopeless an operation. Peas might have been easier, but then I'd need to install some kind of mesh for the vines to climb. Plus, who ever heard of a one-foot long row of peas?

My mother had shown me how to plant peas: make a row of holes in the earth with your finger ("up to the second joint"), about an inch apart. Then drop in the seeds, which looked like little white pills. Cover them and gently pack the earth. She helped me to water them, and a week or two later, sprouts poked through the earth, tiny stems with tiny leaves.

Cherry tomatoes were the only thing that worked that day with my own children. We used actual plants—seedlings I'd bought from Jean-Talon market. After packing the earth around them as if tucking their dolls into bed, Aviva and Alex took turns filling the watering can from the rain barrel and dousing them.

We kept up the vegetable patch for a few years, but I came to accept that gardening is just not my thing. It's not something I enjoy. Plus, squirrels always ate the tomatoes. Alex lost interest. So last fall, when we pulled up the dried-up vines, I put away the climbing stakes for good. I thought Aviva would protest, but there's a vegetable garden at her school now, so I guess she's getting her fix.

I was born on my mother's birthday. I like to think that I was the best birthday present ever. Growing up, I secretly felt it was the one advantage I had over my sisters, making up for all the unfair advantages they seemed to enjoy from having been born five and six years earlier. I loved sharing my birthday cake with my mother on that special October day. To be fair, my sisters did pave the way for a lot of things. Especially my middle sister, Anne. She was the rebellious and adventurous one, going on hiking trips and moving in with her boyfriend at age nineteen.

Still, I was the baby of the family.

One day, well into my mother's illness, I was home alone with her. She called me into her bedroom. Her voice was weak. She was lying on her side, pale. I tried to ignore the blood stains on the crumpled sheets.

"I want you to do something for me," she said. "Go into the bathroom and flush the toilet. Don't lift the lid. Just flush."

"Okay."

I left her room and walked to the bathroom, my heart pounding. It was a big bathroom that we all shared. I didn't know anyone else with such a great bathroom. My father had designed it himself, along with the rest of the house. It had two sinks with large mirrors and lots of counter space for our toothbrushes, soap, lotions and hair brushes, lots of storage space in the cupboards under the sink, and lots of towel racks and hooks. There were no windows but there was a skylight. On sunny days the room was bright, and on rainy days I could hear the patter of raindrops from my room across the hall. There was a full-size bathtub with a shower, and lots of room to dry off. We kept the laundry hamper in the bathroom, too. Right beside the toilet.

Don't lift the lid.

Is it worse to know or to imagine? I'd heard my mother retching. There would be blood. What else? I did not lift the lid. I pushed obediently down on the metal lever. A simple action. My mother had had the strength to close the lid and walk back to her room, but not to flush.

I listened to the water filling and evacuating the bowl in one big, heavy gush. Then the faint drone as the tank slowly and steadily refilled. I walked back to my mother's room but stopped at the doorway.

"I flushed," I said.

"Thank you," she said. She rolled onto her other side and closed her eyes.

It's a scene that has stayed with me all these years. It's a mother's instinct to protect. Don't lift the lid.

I stand behind the front desk of the school library, picking up books from the pile just returned by a Grade 1 class and scanning them one by one into the computer. The children are sitting quietly on the carpet listening to the librarian read a story, but as soon as that finishes, they'll jump up and run to the front desk to take out this week's books.

I volunteer at the library every few weeks, taking turns with other parents. We help with checking the books in and out and shelving them, so the librarian can focus on the children. This morning I'm glad to be occupied by these simple physical tasks. My mind keeps wandering back to an email that my husband forwarded me last night from his friend Paul, who he's known since high school.

"A few months ago, Nathalie was diagnosed with breast cancer," Paul wrote. Nathalie is his girlfriend. "She'll be going into hospital on Friday for a single mastectomy. The doctors are optimistic because they caught the cancer at an early stage. Nathalie is obviously scared but she is being very brave."

Pick up book, scan barcode, listen for beep, check screen to make sure the title appears correctly, place book on cart. Pick up next book.

I don't know Nathalie well. She and Paul started dating a bit over a year ago, after Paul and his wife broke up. She's a university physics teacher and has two teenage kids. The last time I saw her was at a birthday dinner for my husband a few months ago. She was lively, vivacious, laughing at people's jokes, bracelets jingling as she gestured animatedly with her hands. It occurs to me that would have been around the time she received her diagnosis. Had she known that night?

Storytime is over and six-year-olds are swarming the desk. Thoughts of cancer disappear as I smile and say hello to each child, locate their name on the list, and then scan the books into the computer. There are the usual issues of forgotten books, requests to put books on hold and squabbles over the more popular books, which the librarian and I deal with as patiently and gently as possible.

Finally, everyone has their books and the teacher ushers them out the door. The librarian and I have a few quiet moments before the next class to shelve the returns.

The librarian's name is Josie. She is nothing like the frumpy, strict, finger-to-the-lips stereotype. She's energetic and always has a kind word for each child. In her first year at the school she reorganized the entire library, moving books down from the top shelves so that children could actually reach them, culling ancient volumes that hadn't been taken out for years, placing comfy bean bag chairs in corners.

We chit-chat about how the year is going by so fast, it's already May. But my mind is not really on the conversation.

"You seem preoccupied," Josie says.

I stare for a moment at the book I'm about to shelve. I tell her about Nathalie.

"How old is she?" Josie asks.

At a certain point in life, when you hear that someone has a life-threatening disease, you're always doing the math. *She's my age,* or *Wow, he's younger than I am.* Nathalie is in fact a few years older than me. But in the end, does it matter?

Our conversation is interrupted by the next class, sixth-graders with complicated requests for renewals and reserves and returning books but putting them on hold for a friend in another class. At this age the girls tower over the boys. A couple of them look like grown-ups.

As I do my best to respond to their requests, I think of an overdue phone call. I'm supposed to call the health clinic to schedule an ultrasound. It's not that my doctor found anything. It's a routine check. Sort of. He's being cautious. One of my breasts is getting denser. Because of my mother's history, I see him every six months at the Cedar Breast Cancer Clinic. Once a year I get a mammogram. Sometimes he sends me for an ultrasound too. "The mammogram doesn't pick up everything in younger women," he once explained.

Later, when the class has left, Josie tells me about someone she knows who has also just been diagnosed. We start talking about doctors and mammograms, and I mention an anecdote about the Cedar clinic. Josie looks at me, searching.

"Family history," I say.

She asks, "Have you gone for genetic testing?"

It sounds obvious. Find out if you have the mutated gene.

"If the answer is positive, what will you do with that information?" the genetics counsellor had asked.

I mulled that over for a while.

"I know someone who found out she had the gene mutation," Josie says. "She had two sisters. Neither were carriers, but she was. She had a double mastectomy three weeks later. Didn't even think twice, for her it was a no-brainer. Her mother had died of breast cancer and she didn't want to put her kids through what she'd suffered."

I say nothing. I can't imagine taking such drastic action. Having the defective gene doesn't automatically mean you'll get sick. And not having the mutation doesn't grant you immunity. It's all statistics. Probabilities.

I refused the testing.

My mother had inflammatory breast cancer, a rare form of the disease and not necessarily hereditary. Still. Just by my Ashkenazi Jewish background, I'm at higher risk.

A stream of eight- and nine-year-olds is filing into the library, whispering and giggling. My daughter is near the end of the line, carrying her books and her pink glasses case. She smiles and gives me a little wave as she passes the front desk.

I watch her sit cross-legged on the carpet with her friends as Josie introduces the day's story.

Once I heard my father tell someone that my mother had been paranoid about getting cancer and that was why she went on all those health kicks. She started making her own yogurt and granola and various other "health foods" that were foreign at the time to Montreal Jewish families. Then she got cancer.

Does worrying about cancer make you more prone?

Paul's email comes back to me. "She is being very brave." I can't help wondering how brave I would be.

I have not discussed my fears with anyone. Perhaps because acknowledging them makes them more real. Perhaps because I don't know how. That's how I was brought up.

During my mother's illness, I was told only what I needed to know: that she had cancer, a serious disease. That she had to go to the hospital for treatment called chemotherapy. That a relative was coming over to babysit. Maybe that was just the parenting style of the day. Or maybe it was my family. Always practical over emotional. Fact over feeling.

Once, probably not long after my mother had started chemo, I found clumps of her hair in the bathroom garbage can. Large clumps of thick, dark brown hair. As a child, that was scarier to me than anything else.

Beverley was babysitting me. She was a friend of my parents, one of those people I'd known all my life, a familiar fixture in the landscape. I didn't know her that well though, and she knew me only in that way that adults know kids because they've seen you grow up, held you when your parents brought you home as a newborn, helped your mother dress you in your snowsuit when you were a toddler, heard about your exploits at school.

She was downstairs talking on the phone. I was upstairs. She probably thought I was in my room, but I was bored, so I was sitting at the top of the stairs in my favourite spot for eavesdropping. Our house had an open layout. There were no doors on the ground floor, except one to a small bathroom. Sound drifted freely up the stairwell. I didn't know who was on the other end, but she was talking about my mother's illness.

"She's been in and out of the hospital a few times already," Beverley was saying. "And the chemotherapy has been so harsh. She's lost all her hair and she's bone thin."

I couldn't see her, but I pictured her overweight frame stuffed into the rocking chair beside the phone, one hand holding the receiver and the other draped over the armrest. Her voice was loud.

"Well no, I don't think so ... Could be, could be."

I shifted position carefully so the stair wouldn't creak.

"It's just the kids, you know, especially Eve. She's only ten. That's too young to lose a mother."

My breath caught. I sat very still.

A few minutes later I tiptoed back to my room, shut the door very carefully and lay down on my bed.

My mother was going to die.

Stupid, stupid woman, I thought—Beverly. She knew I was in the house. What was she thinking?

And yet. When I think back on that time, it may have been the best thing anyone could have done. Because despite the hospital trips, the ambulances, the bloodied sheets, the sounds of her throwing up, her tears, her spells of weakness, it was the first time I grasped what it all meant: she could die. And from that moment on, some part of me started getting used to the idea. Some part of me started to prepare.

I'm sitting on my son's bed, my back leaning against the wall where a map of the world has been taped and re-taped because it keeps falling down. He has a test coming up. I'm holding his iPad, reading a Power-Point presentation his teacher prepared, and asking him questions about Quebec society in the 1800s. History is his least favourite subject. Mine too.

My son excels at school. He's especially good at math and English. It all comes easily and naturally to him. With history, though, he has to work for it. He doesn't like that.

I was like that as a kid too. Our temperaments are similar. Whereas his sister makes friends within the first hour of being in a new class, he's more withdrawn. He sits and observes. He makes good friends, but it takes time. Again, just like me.

I ask him another review question. I'm impressed with the curriculum. I don't remember learning any of this in fifth grade. All I remember, very vaguely, is the fur trade. My friend Doris and I built this amazing fur trade fort. The fortifying walls were built of popsicle sticks. We made miniature teepees, and Doris crafted little people out of sticky homemade playdough—Indigenous women with babies slung on their backs and men sitting cross-legged around piles of fur and blankets with the Hudson's Bay Company stripes. We spent hours on it.

One day after working on the project at Doris's house, I came home and knelt beside my mother, who was lying on the sofa, to tell her all about it. I described how we'd spray-painted pine cones green to look like evergreen trees.

"That sounds lovely," my mother said. She was too weak to get up. A housekeeper had been hired to do the laundry and cook dinner.

Our fort won an award at a regional school fair.

My mother never got to see it.

There was a five-year rule. After the operation and the chemotherapy, if you lasted five years without a relapse, you were safe. I overheard the adults talking about it.

To my parents, five years would have seemed short. To my childish mind, it was an eternity.

Memory. I remember so little. Fragments. Wisps. And what I don't remember has been filled in over the years with what I've been told or imagined, until memory and imagination have merged into one.

I'm not one for history. I'm not one for dredging up the past. Maybe because it seems pointless—boring details and dates, dead facts that may or may not be relevant but certainly cannot be altered. Life has evolved. Is it not better to focus on the present?

But whenever my son whines and asks why he needs to study history, I always tell him that the past helps us understand the present and plan for the future. So I realize it's time to take my own advice and ask my uncle a few questions. While he's still around to answer them.

My uncle David is a big man, in his late seventies now, but he was once my mom's baby brother. I don't see him often anymore, but a few years ago when I was writing a story about my grandparents, I sat down with him to ask about his family. He mentioned a few details about my mom, but at the time, I didn't pursue it. I didn't ask any questions about her. That seems strange to me now, but maybe I wasn't ready to lift the lid.

My uncle tells me she was a happy person, a smiler. "But she was explosive. When she got upset, she'd flare and get it off her chest immediately. She'd yell and scream and carry on, and then it would be gone." He was the opposite, he said, keeping things inside, not sharing his emotions with anyone.

He describes her as "a big, strapping, strong girl" who was good at everything she did. Not art, though. Even though she went into fine arts, she didn't have the natural talent or artistic drive of her mother. Or of her offspring, as it turns out. One of my sisters is a visual artist, the other a photographer.

My uncle and my mom played well together as children, and as they grew older they fought, as siblings do. "Then somehow after she got married, we went from fighting to becoming the best of friends. Maybe because we weren't in each other's face anymore. She was my guide, my advisor." He pauses. "Really, she was my best friend … until she was gone."

She kept her hair short because she hated fuss. She was down-to-earth, with no patience for airs or falseness. David recalls a visit he made about two weeks after my oldest sister was born. "Your mother said, 'Here, hold her. I gotta go do something. Time you learned how to hold a baby.' I stood there, frozen, with this kid in my hands. I didn't dare move. That was her. Hands-on."

I ask if he sees anything of her in my sisters or me. But deep down, I already know the answer. My older sister is a carbon copy of her, both physically and in character. My middle sister and I, less so, but still. Anne is the most hands-on person I know. She built her own home mostly herself, not to mention that she lives out in the country and has a huge garden. As for me, well … in some ways I'm probably more like my uncle. Keeping all my feelings and stories inside.

I visited my mother in the hospital only once. I don't remember when it was or how long she'd been there. I realize now that it must have been near the end. Had she asked to see me? Had I asked to see her?

She lay on the white hospital bed sheets, looking weak and foreign. I was afraid to go near her. Taped to the window next to her bed was a piece of artwork I'd made at school for Mother's Day. It was a version of stained-glass art, with a picture cut out from black construction paper and coloured cellophane glued onto the back to shine through the holes. I'd made a big sun, bright yellow, shining between the strips of black construction paper, and a house and tree.

She smiled and held out her arms for me to come closer. It was an awkward hug because I didn't want to climb onto the hospital bed. She felt thin. I suspect that she asked me about school and my friends and that I didn't talk much. Who else was there? My father, but others too, I think. After a few minutes I was ushered out of the room.

After she died, I wondered if anyone had taken down that Mother's Day gift, and what they had done with it. In my mind's eye I see the empty hospital bed, stripped of its sheets, and my paper-and-cellophane picture still taped to the window, forgotten, alone in the barren room.

It's end of June, end of school for the kids, and we're spending our first official summer weekend at my husband's parents' cottage near Sutton. It's so hot that I insisted on a family trip to the nearest lake, a half-hour drive. To me, summer only starts after that first plunge into a lake.

Alex flops face-down onto his towel. He likes swimming in pools but is not keen on muddy, algae-infested bodies of water. Aviva is already half-way to the shore, disregarding my calls to wait. I'm digging in my knapsack for my goggles and haven't even pulled my shorts off. She's not allowed in without a grown-up, but it's always been hard to keep her out. I affectionately call her my "little fish."

My mother used to take us to the lake in the old green Ford. The metal seat belt buckles burnt our hands if we left the car in the sun. The front was reserved for grown-ups. The floor on the passenger's side, rusted through so badly you could see the road beneath your feet, was deemed too dangerous for kids. I'd sit in the back between my two sisters, bare thighs sticking to the vinyl seat, a big, squishy beach ball on my lap. I remember the wind rushing in from the open car windows, and the familiar turn of the road into the state park, wheels crunching on gravel as we parked in the dusty lot. We'd gather up our towels and books and bags and carry them down the hill, grass tickling our feet, and my flip-flops would always be sliding off. The challenge was to find a good spot on the lumpy grass, not too close to the garbage cans buzzing with flies and wasps. Then I'd strip off my shorts and flatten my towel before dashing into the lake, pausing only to avoid sharp rocks and mucky patches of algae.

When I was really little, I'd build sand castles with plastic pails and shovels, creating a moat and a channel to the edge of the water.

Eventually, my mother would come down to the shore and wade in slowly, up to her waist. Then she'd slip in without a fuss and swim sidestroke.

Sometimes we'd pad barefoot up to the canteen, feet burning once we got to the hot, painted wooden deck, and we'd order French fries, soft with ruffled edges, salty and warm, served in a rectangular cardboard box. Often my mom would pack a cooler, with peaches or plums. Now, whenever I bite into a ripe, juicy plum, I taste summer.

I finally find my goggles under Alex's book—which I toss in front of him—strip off my shorts and jog down to the lake, weaving around other families and couples sprawled on the grass.

Aviva is already up to her knees. "Mommy, come!" she calls.

"Give me a minute," I say, gasping as my bare skin makes contact with the cold.

"It's fine!" she says.

We wade in until the water is up to her chest. She swims and splashes and jumps, calling on me every two seconds to watch her do this, watch her do that. I oblige. Later we run back to get Daddy, and I manage to coax Alex to join us. We have a ritual in which he and I stand at the edge of the water and yell "One, two, three, go!" Then we run into the water, splashing. The first one to dive under, head and all, wins.

Later, lying on my towel staring up at the blue sky, I ask my husband if he's heard any news about Nathalie since her operation.

He looks up from his Kindle and admits that he hasn't enquired. "But I think she and Paul were in London last week, so she must be doing okay."

I went for my ultrasound last week. But I won't know the results until I see my doctor next month. It's probably fine. I shouldn't worry. But I do. Every time. The anxiety, the waiting, then the relief. A ritual repeated every year, like a charm to ward off something hovering, always potentially around the corner.

My mind turns again to Nathalie, who continues to post pictures on Facebook of special moments with her kids, of dinners and birthday parties and pillow fights. Does she post to share or to preserve? In the end, maybe that's the best we can do. Dive into life. Swim in it. Help others to swim too.

The cliché sounds good in theory.

Aviva and Alex are clamouring to go back into the lake. I sigh, grab my goggles and race them across the sand.

I remember the day she died.

It was a Friday. I was in Grade 5 and my teacher was Mr. H. He was my first male teacher. Mr. H was smart, enthusiastic, and loved to organize field trips. It was one of my best years in elementary school.

That Friday as I was leaving the classroom for my locker, he asked, "So what do you have on this weekend?"

"Going to the country house," I said, shouldering my school bag.

"Some people have all the luck," he said winking, and I left happy.

But when I let myself into the house with my key, something stopped me from shouting out my usual "I'm home!" Maybe I sensed that there were people in the house other than my father and sisters.

My father appeared in the doorway to the vestibule. His eyes were red. "Mom died," he said.

I don't know what happened next. I suppose he gave me a hug, in his awkward way. My uncle David and aunt Sheila were there. Uncle David gave me a hug. That much I know. He was the only one in our family who always gave big hugs.

I sat on the sofa in the living room. My throat was so tight that I could barely swallow. I couldn't talk. I couldn't cry.

In a novel I once read as a teen, a girl is told that her parents are getting a divorce. What she wants to do is take this piece of news back to the privacy of her room like a squirrel with a nut, so that she can examine it and test her teeth on it. But she can't. Instead, she sits at the table with her family as they discuss logistics.

That was probably me. Even though there was nothing preventing me from disappearing to my room. I think I did go eventually, once I'd realized people were too preoccupied to notice.

What happened while I sat there? Where were my sisters? Was my aunt making supper? My aunt must have made us supper.

I didn't cry then, or at the funeral. Years would pass before the tears would finally fall.

There's something I need to do. It's been at the back of my mind for a while now: I need to visit my mother's grave. I've never done this before. Until a few years ago, I didn't even know where it was. That's how much our family talks about these things.

I follow my smartphone's instructions to Kehal Israel Memorial Park, the Jewish cemetery in Dollard-des-Ormeaux, a suburb in the northwestern part of the island of Montreal. I arrive to discover a long narrow strip, not the sprawling endless hills of Mount Royal, or even the endless rows of the Jewish cemetery on De La Savane Street, where my father is buried. I'm also struck by how low the headstones are.

Each section has a gateway formed by two stone pillars, one bearing the name of the congregation in English and the other in Hebrew. I stop the car at Slumber Haven. That can't be the name of a congregation. Maybe it is a section for those lost souls who don't belong to a synagogue.

I follow the caretaker's directions, down four rows and to the left. After all these years of contemplating a visit to my mother's grave, the scene is not quite as I had envisioned. It's not a quiet, peaceful walk with the wind blowing through the trees. In actual fact, heavy metal music is screeching from a house just on the other side of the fence. But at least it's not pouring rain like it was this morning.

I make my way over the grass between the headstones on either side, taking care not to step on anyone's grave.

And then, about halfway down the aisle, I see it:

SARAH LOIS
KRAKOW
October 27, 1936
May 15, 1981

It is a simple grey headstone with a menorah engraved top centre.

And I feel … reassured. Settled. After all these years, all these ephemeral memories, fragments and wisps, here is something tangible. Peace spreads through me, easing the tension in my shoulders.

There's no wave of grief, no nostalgia, no longing. Just a feeling of landing. The realness of the stone is a strange comfort.

My first thought is surprise that she was buried as Krakow, without even a mention of her maiden name, Katz. Was this her choice, specified in her will, a relic of the resentment that David once told me she harboured toward her parents? But her father was still alive when she died. Maybe that's just how it was in those days. She was no longer Sarah Katz. She was a Krakow. Somehow that makes me feel closer to her. I am a Krakow.

My second thought is, why is she buried so close to Betty Bhereur, 1917-1982? Who is Betty Bhereur? A relative? A close friend? The way the graves are placed, they could be husband and wife. It feels sad, like she wasn't important enough to have a space all her own. Of course my father would not have been thinking ahead about his own grave so early in his life. My uncle says my father could barely think at all after my mother died. My aunt and uncle had to make all the funeral arrangements.

Actually, I had expected her to be buried with her parents. But I see no Abraham or Clara Katz. Part of me considers asking the caretaker to check the computer to find out if my grandfather is buried in this cemetery too, but another part of me thinks, no, not today. This is enough.

So here she lies, isolated, on her own among strangers. Of course, the down-to-earth side of me knows perfectly well that once you're dead, it doesn't matter. She would have said the same.

There is a footstone too, framed by the verdant grass, still damp from the rain. It has a Hebrew inscription which I don't know how to read, although I have a vague idea of what it says, a standard phrase in the Jewish tradition.

Then her name appears again, and below it, "Beloved wife, mother, daughter and sister."

I think for a moment of what each of those words represent—especially the word "sister." I hear my uncle's voice in my head: *"She was my best friend ... until she was gone."*

The blaring music has stopped. I sit for a minute on the grass and look around. The sun is hot. I should have sent the kids to camp with sunscreen today after all. The place does not fit my memories of the day of the burial. The trees and hedges are close behind me. Everything seems small and cramped. But there would have been fewer graves in this cemetery back then, and besides, I was seeing through a child's eyes.

I take several pictures with my phone, not just for me but for my sisters, who live far away. To my knowledge, neither of them have been here since the day of the funeral either.

When I started this story, it seemed important to fill in all the gaps. I've filled in a few. The rest don't seem to matter anymore. The knowledge and memories I have, even if imperfect, are enough.

Before I leave, I do one more thing: I take a pebble from my pocket and place it on top of the headstone. It's smooth and purple. I found it at a beach in Newfoundland last year. At the time I picked it up for no other reason than that I liked it, that it felt soft in my hand, and despite my belief that you should leave what you find in nature where it is for others to enjoy, I had allowed myself that one small souvenir. It sat through the winter in a bowl on my dresser. I saw it this morning when I put my ring on. For one selfish second I hesitated because it would mean giving it up, but then I made my decision.

It's Jewish tradition to place a small stone on a grave when you visit. I'm not exactly sure why. I googled it and as with most Jewish traditions, there are multiple theories about its origins and meaning. The explanation I found that makes the most sense to me is that originally, when people were buried, there was no headstone to mark the spot, and so people would place a few stones over the grave. Then, every time they visited, they would add a stone, to make sure the spot remained marked and that the person would not be forgotten.

It's a tradition I love for its simplicity. No flowers, nothing fancy. Just a rock. Just to say, I was here. I haven't forgotten you.

I like to think my mother would have liked that. A stone from the earth. No fuss.

It's midsummer and I've just picked the kids up from day camp. Aviva is bursting at the seams, barely able to contain her excitement. She has something she wants to show me at home, a secret she's been protecting all day, something she discovered just before leaving the house with my husband this morning. She tugs at my arm for the whole ten-minute walk from the metro station, eager to arrive home. When we finally get there, she instructs me to close my eyes. She leads me across the bumpy grass, around to the side of the house. We stop.

"Open!" she says.

I open my eyes. We're standing in front of the spot where we used to have our vegetable patch. It takes me a moment to realize what I'm seeing.

"Tomatoes?" I move closer to examine the mess of green plants.

I can't quite believe it. Amid the weeds, several robust-looking tomato plants are growing. Their stems and leaves unmistakable. Little yellow flowers are blossoming.

I'm sure I pulled up all the dried-up plants last fall. To my knowledge, in Canada, tomatoes are not perennials because the frost kills them. You have to replant every year.

Aviva and Alex start postulating how maybe the seeds from one of the squirrel-bitten tomatoes last autumn replanted themselves. My theory is that some roots were left in the ground, although it's a miracle that they survived the winter.

I can't help wondering if it's a sign.

Life is tenacious. It fights, it goes on. Despite the odds. And we must do the same.

I get down on my knees, feeling the sun-baked dirt on my skin. We set to work, the three of us pulling weeds, making room for the tomatoes to breathe.

PART IV
IN FULL VOICE

Summer Evenings After Dinner

SUMMER EVENINGS AFTER DINNER, my father would ask, "Who's up for a walk?"

Me. Always. We'd walk down the hill, ten city blocks to the magazine store. He never read books, always magazines, with a cigarette hanging off his lip.

My running shoes stuck to the asphalt as we crossed each street. Above me, the leafy green canopy swayed against dark blue sky, street lights just coming on, glowing in the twilight. We didn't talk. Each of us lost in our thoughts, content that way.

* * *

My father did not engage in any sport, but he liked to walk. Stroll. Wander. Meander. Not that he didn't enjoy driving; he drove a lot. Maybe it was just that he liked to move. Go places. The irony is that my children never saw him walk. All they remember is an old man in a wheelchair, or riding his mobility scooter. He was always perched on it precariously, on the verge of falling off. I had to fight the urge to run up and set his body straight. He even rode the scooter in the house, banging into walls. It drove my step-mom crazy.

* * *

I walk everywhere, all the time. I walk to pick up my daughter from school. I walk to the grocery store, pulling my two-wheeled shopping cart behind me. I walk to and from the metro station, to and from the bus stop. I walk to the car-share lot. I walk to the library. I walk to the bagel shop, the pharmacy, the fruit and vegetable store, the coffee shop.

I will look for any excuse to go walk.

* * *

It begins as a dim ache, a few inches below the right buttock, like a pulled muscle. Except that it's not a pulled muscle—that much I can tell. It persists, days, weeks, a month. Sometimes the pain travels down the leg, behind the knee. It's not sharp, but it pulls. Like when I took ballet in Grade 2, and we sat on the floor doing that exercise where you bend your knees, hold your toes, and then stretch your legs out all the way. If you were flexible, once your legs were flat, you were to lean forward as far as you could go, until your nose was touching your knee. But I was not flexible. I could barely straighten my legs. It was the most uncomfortable feeling, the hamstring pulling and pulling.

* * *

I walk to think. Organize my day in my head, plan my week. Work out problems. Come up with ideas.

I walk to clear my head. Or, as they say in French, *se changer les idées*—meaning to replace the ideas in your head with others. One afternoon when I get to a certain intersection, instead of turning left to follow my usual loop, I turn right. What better way to replace the ideas in my head than by walking on different streets?

* * *

After a month, I go see a massage therapist. She does not think the problem is muscular. She advises me to consult a doctor. While she doesn't want to speculate, she tells me of other clients who had similar symptoms. Their diagnoses ranged from a pinched nerve in the spine to thrombosis.

* * *

My father's symptoms began with a stiffness in his leg. The doctor thought he had gout. I thought that gout was a disease that old, rich men got back in the 1800s from eating and drinking too much,

114

something out of one of my English literature books. A few years later, my father was diagnosed with Parkinson's disease. He didn't tell anyone outside of the family. Hid his trembling hands.

* * *

People offer me lifts. I say, "Thanks, but I'll walk."

"Are you sure?" they always ask. "It's raining / hot / cold / far."

"I'm fine," I say.

How to explain that these solitary moments are not just a choice but a need?

* * *

Night. I lie in bed. The pain is still there, faint, but enough. I turn and shift, not wanting to wake my husband but needing to find a more comfortable position. I can't.

* * *

I go through a lot of shoes. They always wear out too quickly, the soles thinning unevenly until my feet hurt. On running shoes, my big toe starts to poke out the fabric. My winter boots start to leak, the damp innocuous at first, then becoming insidious, the cold gripping my whole foot until it feels locked in ice.

* * *

The doctor examines my leg. Asks me question after question. There's no obvious diagnosis, so she suggests an X-ray. "It's a place to start," she explains. No appointment needed, and it's covered by Medicare.

* * *

When I was young, our family travelled. Across the border and down the coast, driving through Vermont, Maine, New Hampshire,

Massachusetts. Once as far as South Carolina. Twice we flew to Europe. And when we got there, we walked. We walked and walked, through the streets of Lisbon, Toledo, Madrid. In Paris, we climbed the spire of the Notre-Dame cathedral. The youngest of three girls, I was three years old on the first trip, five years old on the second. It was the early 1970s. When I got tired, my father hoisted me onto his shoulders.

* * *

I tell my doctor the pain hasn't gotten worse, but later realize that's not true. It has definitely gotten worse. More present, more constant. Taking hold. Like a photograph lying in a bath of developer in my father's basement darkroom, the picture becoming solid. Black areas growing darker against the white, the contrast sharpening, contours becoming more defined. The pain is always there now, not acute, but a continuous discomfort, in want of relief.

* * *

I walk the streets of Montreal. My home city, city that I love. I walk past duplexes and triplexes with their iconic outdoor staircases, past bicycles locked to fences, past green and blue recycling bins overflowing with flattened cereal boxes and empty juice cartons. I walk along tree-lined streets bursting with bright reds and golds in the fall. I kick through snowdrifts in the winter. I walk downtown among the shadows of tall buildings, glancing at the window displays of shoes and clothing and books, at couples sitting in coffee shops. I walk past other people walking, behind other people, in front of other people, among other people, walking.

* * *

Bit by bit, I learned about Parkinson's. A progressive nervous system disorder that affects movement. It manifests itself differently in different people, and the rate of progression can vary. Common symptoms include tremors, slowed movement, rigid muscles, impaired balance and coordination, and speech changes. There's no cure, although drugs can alleviate symptoms and possibly slow the disease's progress.

* * *

To my surprise, something does show up on the X-ray. "*There is a slight wavy periosteal bone reaction along the posterior aspect of the upper femur,*" the report states. "*Quite a nonspecific finding.*" I ask my doctor what could be causing this bone reaction, but it's too "nonspecific" for her to offer any hypotheses.

My doctor requests an MRI for within 28 days. When I call the hospital's imaging centre, a voice message tells me there's a wait time of six months. Appointments will be given according to priority level. I doubt they'll consider my case a priority. But it's becoming a priority for me.

* * *

Sometimes my father's walk was very determined. Like at the country house, when he took those long, purposeful strides across the grass runway toward one of his remote-controlled model airplanes. I can still see him crouching down to adjust a wing flap. Scents of sweet clover and cut grass mingle with the smell of engine grease. He used to fly real planes, gliders, before my older sister was born. I grew up watching him stand in the field with a remote controller in his hands, thumbs on the levers, eyes on the sky.

Out in the country, I learned to walk along the road. A highway. Always face the traffic, I was told. We'd walk up the hill to the Red Store and Ashery, converted into a gift shop with an old-fashioned penny-candy counter. It was a tiring trek for my child-size legs, but the reward was strings of red licorice, chewy Tootsie rolls, cherry jujubes, round peppermint chocolates and Icy Squares that melted sweet and cool on the tongue.

* * *

I walk to be a part of this world.

117

* * *

The pain pulls at the back of my thigh, an insistent reminder. Tugging, like a child begging for attention. Sometimes when I sit, it radiates through my whole leg, like when you hit your funny bone, only more muted. A taut wire vibrating. Something just on the edge.

The "what ifs" begin. What if it's not just an injury, a torn ligament, a "mechanical" problem. What if it's something more insidious. A cancer eating away at the bone marrow. A degenerative disease. It's already progressed considerably in such a short period of time. What if I have to limit my activities. Stop walking to my daughter's school, stop walking to the grocery store, avoid any unnecessary walking. What if it's permanent. My new normal. What if my condition deteriorates.

(What if I can't walk anymore.)

* * *

In his last years, my father couldn't walk at all. Imprisoned in a body reduced, crippled, controlled by the disease. Stubbornly insisting on riding his mobility scooter when we were all sure he'd either fall off or run someone over. He could hardly control his hands anymore to work the levers. Hardly see to navigate.

* * *

Last spring, my daughter fractured her ankle. She had to wear a cast for five weeks. Five weeks of crutches. No more walking to school or even taking the bus. No walking anywhere. She wanted to, she tried, but three blocks was about her limit with the crutches. Thank goodness it's not winter, we said. Thank goodness it won't ruin your summer, we said. The cast was removed on her last day of school. She wasn't able to put any weight on her leg for a while; the muscles had atrophied. But the very next day, a hot summer Saturday, we went to the pool. She abandoned her crutches on the edge and swam free, like a fish let loose from a net. "I feel like a real person again," she said.

* * *

I cannot wait six months. Fortunately, my husband's insurance through his job will cover an MRI at a private clinic. I call. They offer me an appointment for the next day.

I enter the room in my hospital gown. There's a steady background thumping, like a washing machine. The tube itself, occupying the centre of the room, is much wider than I imagined. My shoulders relax and I exhale.

I lie down, head on a pillow. The technician arranges a blanket around me. It's warm and comfortable. She places a large slab-like device on my middle. Slides me in. Not all the way since it's just for my leg. I stare up at the edge of the tube, at a row of lights. It's very futuristic.

The technician gave me ear plugs and ear muffs, along with a warning, but the noise is still much louder than I expect. A high-pitched buzz, beeping, then a series of pulses, honks, as if someone forgot to turn off their car alarm. I count four groups of four beats, like four measures of music in 4/4 time, first high, then low. I can feel heat around my knees. I'm dying to lift my head to see, but I was told not to move.

What will happen after I get the MRI results? Probably more tests, to make a diagnosis. Blood tests, maybe.

* * *

The "what ifs" grow and loom. Like shadows in a children's bedroom, morphing into monsters with jagged teeth and hungry eyes.

* * *

Toward the end, my father couldn't even ride his scooter. He spent most of his time in his room at the nursing home. Had to rely on other people to push him around in his wheelchair.

* * *

The phone rings. A glance at the call display tells me it's my doctor. She never calls, usually waits for my appointment. My heartbeat quickens.

"I have the MRI report," she says. "Tendonitis."

That's it? Tendonitis? Almost a let-down.

"There's inflammation," she says, "of the tendon attached to the gluteus maximus."

I nearly burst out laughing. Gluteus maximus. It sounds made-up, a character from an *Asterix* comic book.

She recommends physiotherapy. I ask if there's anything I should or shouldn't do, movements I should avoid, but she just says she'll mail me the referral.

* * *

My father had a very distinct gait. He didn't just walk, he bounced. My sisters and I could recognize his walk from a mile away. Now, I like to indulge myself in thinking each step was, in some way, a bounce of joy. An unconscious tic revealing his joie-de-vivre. Or that each step was a leap toward flying, reigned in only by the gravity of the Earth itself.

The New Door

THIS IS THE YEAR we get a new front door. It's needed replacing ever since we moved in six years ago, but this summer the old wood warped in the relentless heat and now it requires a full-body shove to close. In winter, snow blows in through the cracks, settling on the carpet in white drifts.

At some point while we were poring over catalogues and discussing frames and hinges and handles, the question struck me: when we have the new door, will we put up a mezuzah?

A mezuzah is that little rectangular box you see affixed at an angle on Jewish people's doorposts. For many, it's mostly symbolic. A tradition they don't even think about. Nearly every Jewish home has one.

Nearly.

There was none on our door when I was growing up. I associated mezuzahs with religious Jews, or at least those who were more observant than I was. Like my friend Sandra, who didn't keep kosher and didn't observe Shabbat, but who stayed clear of bread on Passover and who fasted on Yom Kippur.

When my husband and I moved into this house, there was already a mezuzah on the door from the previous owner. We left it there. "I wouldn't put one up, but I'm not going to take it down if it's there," my husband said. I felt the same way.

But now, since we will be taking it down to replace the doorframe, will we put it back?

Ten years ago I wouldn't have even considered the question. Now, it's a dilemma. Why?

I know why. Because of my in-laws. Because of my kids. Maybe even because of my own past.

I didn't grow up in a religious home. Yes, we lit candles on Chanukah, attended Passover Seders led by my grandfather or aunt, and stayed home from school on Rosh Hashanah and Yom Kippur. But the only time I ever set foot in a synagogue was to attend a wedding. We ate shellfish and pork. *Matzah* and bread sat side by side on the kitchen counter during the eight days of Passover.

I attended public schools, English Protestant and French Catholic (back in the days of denominational school boards in Quebec). My friends were Greek, Chinese, Indian, Hungarian. As a young adult, I celebrated Christmas with my French boyfriend.

Yet now I live in a predominantly Jewish neighbourhood, within walking distance of three synagogues. My kids went to a Jewish pre-school and go to summer camp at the Jewish "Y" down the street. In winter, we attend Sunday storytime at the Jewish Public Library. On Friday mornings I stop in at the kosher bakery to get a *challah*, and on Friday evenings we enjoy Shabbat dinners at my in-laws'.

How did this happen?

I blame my son.

My husband and I were living in a small rented apartment on De Gaspé Avenue, in Montreal's Little Italy. It was a Friday morning, and I was about to call our real estate agent to place a bid on a duplex we'd seen in the mostly francophone district of Villeray. But at thirty-four weeks pregnant, I was tired and decided to lie down for a bit first. When I got up, a trickle of clear liquid was running down my leg. My water had broken.

My son was in the neonatal intensive care unit for ten days. He turned out fine, but we dropped the whole house-hunting business for several months. Then, with the new perspective of freshly minted parents, we accepted the proposal of my husband's parents to buy and live in a duplex together.

Or maybe it began before that. When, lying on our backs in bed during our first night together, the man who would later become my husband asked me, "What religion are you, anyway?"

I turned my head to look at him, surprised. "Jewish, of course. I thought you knew."

He started laughing.

I had known he was Jewish. How could I not, with that hair, that nose, and that surname? I had assumed it obvious in my case too.

He was laughing because neither of us had ever imagined we'd end up dating a Jew.

When searching for a duplex together, my in-laws wanted to be within walking distance of a synagogue; we needed a metro station. We ended up in Snowdon, a residential yet central neighbourhood of tree-lined streets and parks. We live downstairs, they live upstairs. Our children, now old enough to climb up and down the connecting spiral kitchen stairwell on their own, consider the entire duplex their home, and say "Mommy-Daddy-Bubby-Zaida" (Grandma and Grandpa) in the same breath.

My in-laws keep a kosher home, attend synagogue on religious holidays, bless the wine and the bread on the Sabbath, use different dishes on Passover. They would never be without a mezuzah on *their* door.

So far they have tolerated our non-religious ways.

Yet it seems, by unspoken mutual consent, they have taken on the role of educating our kids about Jewish religion and culture. They involve them in the blessings and rituals, bring them to synagogue on major holidays, and give them menorah- and dreidel-shaped cookie cutters for our "holiday" baking.

Part of me is grateful and appreciative. For I wonder, if we had ended up on our own in Villeray, our kids at the local public school, visiting their grandparents once every week or two, what would we have done to pass on their Jewish heritage? Would we have celebrated the Jewish holidays? Would I have felt a need to counter-balance the Catholicism around us? Really, my in-laws are making it easy for me.

But sometimes, discomfort nags at my consciousness. Part of me resents the subtle nudges, even though they are made with love and good intent. Part of me would rather just use our traditional cookie cutters, the heart and crescent moon and animal shapes, and so what if there's a Christmas tree too?

I ask my husband what he thinks about the mezuzah.

"When we change the door, are we going to put one back up?"

"I wasn't planning to," he says.

"Do you think your parents will mind?"

He frowns and nods his head vigorously. "Oh yeah."

We have our own mezuzah somewhere, a wedding gift. Perhaps I should look for it.

On the day before Rosh Hashanah, the Jewish New Year, I was explaining to my six-year-old son that he'd go to *shul* (synagogue) with Bubby and Zaida on the first day of the holiday, but that on the second he'd go to school as usual. I added that Daddy and I would be working both days.

"But not Bubby and Zaida," he said.

"That's right."

"Because Bubby and Zaida are more Jewish than we are," he said.

I debated explaining the concepts of "observant" or "religious" or "practising," but as usual, it is the child who sums it up best.

What is the meaning of the mezuzah? I search the Internet, clicking on MyJewishLearning.com, *Judaism 101* (jewfaq.com), the *Jewish Virtual Library*—sites intended for clueless Jews like me.

But the ambivalent Jew in me wants to have a genuine conversation. I take a deep breath and, for the first time since my wedding, set up a meeting with a rabbi. (We had wanted a secular wedding at city hall, but in the face of my in-laws' desolation, had agreed to a small ceremony at their home, led by a rabbi.)

Up until a few years ago, I never realized that the mezuzah is really all about the scroll inside; the box is just a case. The scroll contains specific passages from the Torah (Old Testament) and from the Shema, one of the basic Jewish prayers.

"The Shema is more of a credo than a prayer," says Rabbi Ron Aigen, as we sit together in his study at the Reconstructionist Synagogue in Hampstead. Two walls are lined with books; a third is covered in diplomas and posters for cultural events. He opens a book and goes over each phrase: "You shall love the Lord your God with all your soul … repeat these words to your children … speak of them at home and when you go out … so that your days and the days of your children may be many upon the land ..." He explains how these words embody the greater, underlying notions of love, continuity, passing on the Jewish tradition to our children, living these values in all aspects of our lives, and aspiring to be a free people.

"The words in the casement, the words of mezuzah, are far-reaching," he concludes. "They refer to the Jewish heritage as a whole."

"Do you think most Montreal Jews today are aware of what the mezuzah really means?" I ask.

"I think for the vast majority of people, mezuzah simply means it's a Jewish home," he says. Not even necessarily a religious home, he adds.

And to Rabbi Aigen, that is perfectly fine: rituals and traditions still have meaning even if you're not religious. "It still has cultural significance," he says.

When I was little, my strongest link to my Jewish heritage was my grandfather, my mother's father.

I remember him as very old-fashioned, always in a grey three-piece suit. In winter he wore some kind of Russian wool hat, and he spoke with a thick Russian (or perhaps Yiddish) accent, even though he'd lived in Canada since the age of ten.

I loved my grandfather; I was his little girl. I remember sitting on his lap, his knees bony under his wool pants. I remember making him play "house" with me, and pushing him onto the sofa to make him sit. He responded with a bemused little laugh, as if to say, "Anything for my little girl," or perhaps, as I've often thought of my own children, "What nature of creature is before me?" I must have been about three.

He was devoutly religious, kept kosher and attended synagogue. He had firm traditional beliefs and opinions. He vehemently disapproved of my elder sister's non-Jewish boyfriend, and threatened to disown her if they got married. But he was kind and generous. When my sisters were in high school and their orchestra was planning a trip to Europe, he helped cover the costs, to be sure they could go.

Rituals and traditions. I remember, as a small child, squirming restlessly in my seat during the interminable Passover Seders he led at our house. He'd tell the whole story first in Hebrew and then again in English so that my sisters and I would understand. Later, we'd hunt for the *afikoman*, the piece of matzah the adults hide for children to find at the end of the meal in exchange for a prize.

I remember my mother chopping prunes to make *hamantashen*, the triangular fruit-filled cookies you eat on Purim. I remember her lighting the Chanukah candles with us, singing the blessing on each of the eight nights.

These memories are part of who I am.

I did attend one year of Jewish school: kindergarten. I once asked my father why. He couldn't remember. Possibly because it offered longer hours than the public school and a day care service. "Or," he said, "maybe we woke up one morning and decided it might be a good idea if you got some Jewish education under your belt."

If so, it worked. Remnants of Hebrew songs remain embedded in my mind. It's where I met Sandra, my best and only Jewish friend for years. It created a foundation, adding to the strata laid by my grandfather and my mother, deep in my consciousness.

It also influenced my decision to send my own kids to a Jewish preschool. Although I could, once again, blame my son.

He was almost five and ready for more than day care. But his birthday would be after the cut-off date for kindergarten, and there was no pre-k at the school we wanted to send him to.

Then I discovered a program at the same Jewish school I had attended, just down the street. It offered a good balance of formal instruction, free play and physical activities. It had an excellent reputation. And it would be refreshing not to be bombarded with Christmas colouring pages and Easter crafts.

My in-laws were ecstatic. "It's just for this year," we said in warning. "He's not staying there."

The thing is, I want my children to be exposed to other cultures and backgrounds from an early age. In my mind, this is the key to being comfortable with others, to understanding them, to having a broad worldview. To achieving personal harmony as well, so that you feel like you can go anywhere, communicate and fit in.

And yet, one could argue that if you don't have a strong sense of your own roots, you may never fit in anywhere. Montreal is home to a large, vibrant Jewish community, which acts as a social, professional and assistance network. It has tradition and pride. Yet when I enter a Jewish institution, I feel as if I don't quite belong.

I find our mezuzah in a box of miscellaneous items still unwrapped from our move. It is in two tones of dark brown and reddish wood, separated by a thin curvy gold line, with the W-shaped Hebrew letter Shin near the top. I run my fingers over the smooth surface, then turn it over and try to decipher the artist's signature carved into the wood.

A mezuzah on your door announces that you're Jewish. "What's wrong with that?" my father-in-law might say—although he'd be the first to point out the prejudice that is still ingrained in our society. Perhaps it comes down to how you define yourself. I consider myself a writer, a singer, a mother, a Montrealer, a Québécoise, a Canadian. I am Jewish, yes, but it comes after many other qualifiers.

My meeting with the rabbi has given me a greater understanding of my in-laws' beliefs. But they are not my beliefs.

Is my house a Jewish home? Yes, by default. But I would like to hope that the values we try to live by—love, understanding, freedom, education, helping those less fortunate—extend beyond religion and heritage.

We still have a few weeks before the new door arrives. For now, I place the mezuzah back in its box.

Contact

I'M SITTING IN FRONT of my computer at home, working. My mind is focused on translating French ideas into English. Brain assembling logical sentences, fingers typing the words. A breeze filters in from the window behind me.

A sound.

Sudden and loud. Metal vehicle coming into contact with …?

My fingers freeze. The screen blurs.

"Oh my god! Oh my god!" a woman screams.

My heart lurches. I'm on my feet, out the door. Dreading. What will I see? A child's mangled body? A mother sobbing?

"Oh my god!" Again.

I race down my front steps. Wanting to see, to know.

Not wanting to see or know.

Over there. A woman sits upright in the middle of the street. Bicycle near her, front wheel pointing up at the sky. Still spinning.

Relief washes over me. It's not a child, but a grown woman. Conscious. She's even wearing a bike helmet.

A man is trying to help her up. The door to a red Toyota hangs open. At the side of the road. Parked.

She's crying, yelling at him. He's apologizing.

"I don't understand. I looked. I checked my mirrors," he says, over and over. "I'm a cyclist too."

Another woman has stopped and taken out her phone. She dials 911. She looks vaguely familiar. A neighbour?

The man helps the cyclist to the sidewalk. She looks about thirty. She sits on the curb, dabs at the tears and blood with shaking fingers. The man goes back to retrieve her bike.

I run back into the house. Rummage for an ice pack and clean cloth. Heart pounding, adrenaline pumping. Thoughts of concussions and internal bleeding swirl around my brain. I moisten the cloth and fill a cup with water. Grab my phone and race back out.

"Hi," I say. I sit down beside her and tell her my name. "I live right there"—turning to the red-brick duplex behind us—"... so if there's anything I can do ..."

"Thanks." She accepts the cloth and ice pack. Brushes away wisps of blond hair that have escaped her ponytail. Holds the ice pack to her face.

I hand her the water.

"No! 911 said don't give water!" the other woman says. Still holding the phone to her ear.

"Sorry," I say.

The driver's girlfriend is here now. It's her car. He was just moving it because of the parking restrictions.

The cyclist's name is Jacqueline. She's already apologizing for yelling at him. She was just scared. Her voice and hands are still trembling, but the blood on her face is just from a cut on the bridge of her nose. From her sunglasses.

I offer her my phone but she has her own. She's talking to someone now. Maybe a friend, or a spouse.

I'm not sure if my presence beside her is comforting or intrusive. I stand up to give her space.

The ambulance arrives and two paramedics take over. One, a man, asks her to describe what happened. He asks her to "move your hand like this" and "now like this" and prods her while the other, a woman, holds Jacqueline's head immobile with two latex-gloved hands.

Jacqueline tells them she's from Calgary but moved in up the street a few weeks ago.

Some welcome to Montreal, I think. At least everyone is being helpful and the paramedics are speaking to her in English.

Two police officers arrive. They question the driver, Jacqueline and the other woman, who witnessed the accident. They examine the bike.

I linger. Feeling extraneous but also like I should stay.

The paramedics and police officers inform Jacqueline that, even though she seems okay, she should still see a doctor. In case a problem develops later, and she wants to make an insurance claim. As the paramedics secure her onto a stretcher, one of the police officers asks Jacqueline what she wants to do with her bike.

"You could leave it with me," I say. Point again at my house. "Come get it whenever."

Jacqueline agrees and we exchange email addresses on bits of scrap paper.

I can't concentrate on anything.

I stare out the window at the cars driving down my tree-lined street. I think back to those first instants this morning. When I raced out. Not knowing what I'd find.

What caused me, really, to rush outside? A genuine desire to help? Or that ugly thirst that makes us slow down on the highway to gawk at an accident? Deep down, there was an almost perverse sense of wanting there to be a crisis so I could be the one to help. But why? To be some kind of hero? No; I'm not good in crisis situations. Not a "people person." I don't think quickly on my feet. Was it some sense of needing a purpose, of wanting to be part of something larger than life, a life and death situation, a crisis that makes you feel alive?

I write an email to Jacqueline to confirm my address. I say I hope she's okay and invite her to come get her bike whenever, no rush. Then I go to the kitchen in search of a snack.

Opening the fridge, I wonder what brought Jacqueline here from Calgary. What she does for a living, if she's single. For some reason, I doubt she has kids. She said she lives just up the street. It would be nice to get to know her. Maybe we'll chat when she comes to get her bike. Maybe this will be the start of one of those friendships where we tell people, twenty years from now, "We met that day she got doored on the street in front of my house ..."

My hand lands on an apple. I'm reminded of the woman who sits cross-legged on the floor at our metro station, every day, head bowed behind a sign that says, "Money or Food. Anything Helps. God Bless." I keep meaning to bring her apples. Sometimes I give her money, sometimes food. I have this fantasy where, one day, I sit down on the floor beside her and she tells me her life story. I ask her what kind of food she likes and if she has a warm coat for the winter. I figure out how to make her life a little easier in some small way. But in real life, I'm too embarrassed. Too shy to say anything more than a mumbled "hi." And in real life, knowing leads to responsibility. Is that why no one stops to ask? Yet I want her to know that I think about her. To connect with her on a basic human level.

Cool water splashes my hands as I rinse the red and green fruit in the sink. Is that it?

Maybe that desire to be able to intervene and to help is really about wanting to connect: wanting to connect with someone on a basic level, in a situation that frees you from the rules that normally govern societal interactions. A situation that exists outside the box of daily conventions.

My doorbell rings. Jacqueline is standing on the doorstep. She's wearing a peach-coloured button-up blouse and grey pants. Her hair hangs loose around her shoulders.

She looks different from what I remember. But of course last time I saw her, she was sweaty and bleeding. I ask how she is and she replies that other than a few scrapes and bruises, she's fine.

I fetch her bicycle, rolling it over from the hallway.

"Thanks again for hanging on to this," she says, as she takes it from me.

"No problem at all," I say. "I'm just glad you're okay."

She's already out the door and on the landing.

"Do you need help carrying it down the stairs?"

"No, I'm good. Thanks again!"

I stand there, watching her carry the bicycle down the steps. At the bottom, she adjusts her purse. Mounts the bicycle.

Rides off.

Long after she turns the corner, I continue to stand there, reluctant to close the door on the morning breeze.

Writer Emerging

As a child, you explore. You wander through brush and tall grass and wild flowers. You run through the field of hay, its tips swaying above your head. You climb the hill, running shoes sliding on the muddy slope. You rest underneath a pine tree on its bed of soft needles, sticky with sap, and breathe in their scent. You look for garter snakes in the rock pile, poking with a stick and peering under stones. You wade into the blackberry bushes to pick large, dark berries, trying to avoid the thorns that catch at your clothes and scratch your bare skin. The sour-sweet juice fills your mouth and stains your fingers purple.

You dare yourself to splash cold water on your face from the fast-moving creek.

You slip your palm gently under the soft belly of a frog, its throat bulging in and out with silent breaths, and wait patiently for it to reposition itself on your hand. You lift your hand ever so slowly and admire the frog's shiny wet skin, until its powerful legs push off from your palm and it jumps back into the water with a loud plop.

It is late summer, and you've been roaming the fields all morning. You perch on a rock beside the creek and force yourself, for a moment, to sit still.

Moss-covered rocks poke up from the water. The current swirls and gurgles around them with smooth purpose.

Measures of birdsong float over the high steady trill of crickets.

Young trees lean in. In the shade of their green canopy, your hot, sticky skin cools and goosebumps form on your arms.

You take several deep breaths. The air smells of dry grass and wild flowers, and tastes of wet earth.

And you are acutely aware, with an insight that marks a sudden awareness of your own childhood, that this is a moment to hold on to.

You have always been writing.

You write poems and stories. You keep a diary. You compose songs. You memorize all the words to the Beatles' song "Paperback Writer." One day your father brings home a stencil machine that a commercial tenant left behind. It's just like the one your teachers use at school. You publish your own newspaper, inhale the glorious smell of fresh blue ink.

You write a book about a girl's search to find her best friend who moved without leaving a forwarding address. Inspired by one of your own friends who has changed schools. The lines of the thick spiral notebook fill with your ten-year-old handwriting. Longing bleeds in your heart but you are not yet able to translate it to the page. It is a longing for true, indissoluble friendship, like in the books you read. You're undecided on what should happen when the girls are reunited at the end. At first, you want them to hug as if they will never part again. But you know that in fiction, as in real life, the girls will have both grown (you sense the meaning of a character arc before you learn the term) and moved on.

As a teenager, you join a theatre group where young people help write the scripts and direct the shows. You submit a script for their summer festival. The play is called *Tightrope*. It is chosen and performed. It's about a boy who is shy and socially inept and so takes refuge in drawing and his own fantasy world. The real world is so difficult for him that he starts to slip into his imaginary universe, confusing the two worlds, losing all sense of reality, losing himself—until some classmates rescue him.

As a young adult, you write a story where the worlds of an introverted painter—the real world around him and the imagined landscapes he paints—begin to blur into one. Again, it is a friend who rescues the main character. He convinces the painter to open up to the world by exhibiting his artwork.

It is some time before you notice the parallels between the two stories—along with others you've written. Writing is your means of expression, your way of communicating with the world. And yet, you feel trapped. You long for ... something. Deep down, you recognize that only you can rescue yourself.

"Thank you for allowing us the opportunity to consider your story titled --- . We have reviewed your work carefully and unfortunately your writing does not meet our needs at this time."

In the safety and secrecy of your head, you conduct interviews to celebrate the (imaginary) publication of your (imaginary) book.

"Why do you write?" the interviewer asks.

"To hold onto life," you say. "To capture those ephemeral, fleeting moments that disappear and dissolve like wisps of smoke. To leave a trace. To reveal hidden beauty and compassion."

When you get older, you add, "To remember." Because whenever you reread stories from earlier years, you are startled by how much you've forgotten.

"Thank you for sending us --- for consideration in --- .I am sorry to say ..."

"While we weren't able to accept your work for publication at this time, we hope ..."

The desks have been arranged in a circle, corners touching. The classroom smells of pencils and chalk and sneakers. Legs are sprawled out beneath the desks and students chew the ends of their pencils in boredom. You wonder how many are taking this creative writing class because they want to write versus how many figure it'll be an easy two credits.

You've been studying Hemingway. The teacher has shown how Hemingway never tells what a character is feeling. He just describes their actions. He writes in direct sentences and uses the word "and" to create long sentences that in other situations would beg for commas and gerunds. Your assignment was to write a short piece imitating Hemingway's style.

Students take turns reading out their pieces. Most have written about bull-fighting and fishing, which they know nothing about but which seems to be all Hemingway wrote about.

You can't help thinking they've missed the point.

You wrote about the day your mother died.

Looking back, you don't remember why. Maybe the teacher said to write about an important moment in your life. Or maybe it was just because you wanted to.

You've never written about her death before. It's been seven years. Last night you sat at your desk in your bedroom and tried to remember.

It's your turn. You start to read. *"They ate late that night. It would not have been right to order out and they weren't very hungry anyway ..."*

A hot blush spreads across your cheeks, as it always does when you become the focus of attention.

Your story is four pages long, handwritten on loose leaf, single-spaced. It's in the third person and your character's name is Cathy.

You reach the last few lines.

"Cathy got up and went to her room. She sat down on her bed. The room seemed empty. The door was closed. She was alone and she was very scared."

You stop.

There is stunned silence.

You don't know how to react to the stunned silence.

Are your classmates just shocked by the personal nature of the story or are they genuinely moved? You suspect they feel a bit sheepish now with their stories of bull-fighting and fishing.

You stare down at your page.

The teacher extols your use of Hemingway's techniques to tell your own story. When the bell finally rings, as you're leaving the classroom, a few students tap your arm and tell you it was a good story.

You have not yet realized the power you wield.[*]

---

[*] Definition of "realize":
1. To become fully aware of (something) as a fact; to understand clearly
2. To cause to happen
3. To achieve (something desired or anticipated); to fulfil
4. To give actual or physical form to
5. *Music*: to add to or complete (a piece of music left sparsely notated by the composer)
6. To convert (an asset) into cash

"We appreciated the chance to read your work. We will not be including your submission in the upcoming issue, but we wish you ..."

A literary journal wants to publish one of your stories. It's a 750-word piece based on a chance encounter with a guy you had a crush on in high school. It reflects all the restlessness and dissatisfaction you have been feeling in life.

Have been. Past tense. At this moment you are running and jumping around the apartment yelling, "Yes! Yes! Yes!"

"We apologise for the delay in response. Unfortunately, this particular piece is not right for ..."

"We are unable to accept your work for publication this time around ..."

Your son is born five weeks early. You sit in the hospital pumping milk from your breasts while he sleeps in an incubator in the intensive care unit. You are exhausted. Overwhelmed. Aching in every part of your body. Then, sitting on the edge of the hospital bed, tears running down your cheeks, you have the very deliberate thought: I will write about this later. This idea gets you through the hours.

And you do write about it. Sixteen months later, while visiting your sister in California. You sit at the computer in her family room, typing, while your son sleeps in his port-a-crib.

You cannot type fast enough.

"We considered your submission carefully, but I'm sorry to say it isn't a good fit for us at this time ..."

"... Unfortunately, the piece is not right for us at this moment ..."

You submitted a story to an anthology on shyness, based on diary entries from your teenage years in the theatre group, and it was accepted. This is your first publication in a book.

When your copies arrive in the mail, you weigh the book in your hands. Two teddy bear eyes peer out from the shiny cover, the word "SHY" in thin white capitals over a dark red background. You consult the table of contents and flip to the page with your story. There's your name, in black capital letters. You run your fingers across the smooth paper.

You feel like a writer.

And yet, you feel guilty, like an imposter, because the story is drawn from material you wrote ages ago and that feels like cheating.

"Thanks for sending us your story. We're sorry to say ..."

"... we will not be able to include your essay in our anthology ..."

Someone is interviewing you for real. You met Nicole at a writing conference and took one of her online courses. She was warm and generous and has become a mentor. Now she's gathering information to develop a new writing course.

You talk over Skype. It's a backwards January day, with snow in Vancouver and ice-rain in Montreal.

After chatting for a bit and discussing writing in general, Nicole pops the question.

"What is your biggest fear?"

Your head swirls. Your blood races. Outside your window, the birch tree's branches look like they are encased in glass. Beautiful but deadly.

You have many fears about your writing: that it's not good enough. That you peaked early and won't get anything else published. That you'll never finish your collection of stories. That you will, but that no one will be interested in reading it.

That your writing leaves you too exposed.

What you say is, "That I'll always be just an emerging writer."

Nicole looks away from the camera for a moment, at the snow in her own yard. There was just enough for her daughter to build a small snowman this morning. She turns back to you.

"I think of being a writer as a way of seeing and understanding the world," she says.

And in that moment, you know her words to be true.

"Writing is my way of processing life," you say to her, but also to yourself. Not so much a revelation as something you've always known, translated into words.

You recall climbing the hill behind the country house, running shoes seeking hold on the muddy slope. The sweet taste of ripe blackberries, the sting of brambles scratching your legs. Your hands cupping cold water from the creek, splashing your hot, flushed face.

You remember the vulnerability of the frog's soft, slippery belly in your palm.

The surprising power of its tiny legs as it leapt off, back into the water.

The Girl in the Khaki Miniskirt

It happens to most people at some point: a blast from the past. You run into someone you haven't seen for years, maybe ten, maybe twenty, and you are jolted back to another time, another life.

Or maybe it comes in the form of an email.

Hi there, it's Sean!

Which Sean? From Young Expressions, of course! I've been trying to find you for ages! I have a stack of your old letters next to me on my computer desk. I see by your profile photo that you have two young children. I'd love to hear what else you're up to these days.

Best wishes,

Sean

P.S. Have you seen the YES Facebook page? Check it out!

My insides jump a mile high when I see the message. Sean. Young Expressions. I lean back in my desk chair.

Young Expressions, or YES as we called it back then, was a performing arts group I joined as a teen. It gave me the chance to act, to sing, and even to write. But it did so much more than that. It was a magical place, far, far away from the dinginess of high school. YES gave me a chance to rid myself of the awkwardness that clung to me like a parasite when I walked down the school halls. YES was a refuge, a fresh start. Sitting on the carpeted floor that first day at the rehearsal space in an old warehouse, listening to the director as she also sat on the floor in front of us talking to us as equals, I could sense a turning point. The beginning of something new.

There, I met people I never would have spoken to otherwise. Kids of all ages and all backgrounds came together. Poor kids, rich kids. Kids who didn't fit the mould. Together, we created shows about racism, the nuclear arms race, domestic violence, teen suicide. I spent every weekend at Young Expressions, and then my entire summer. Our rehearsal space felt more like home than my real home. In my last year of high school, I was even chosen to be part of the group's European Tour.

Then I started college, made new friends, found my first boyfriend. Eventually I left YES behind, shedding it like a sweater I'd outgrown.

And now, twenty years later, a message.

I visit the YES Facebook page. I scan the group member names, recognizing about half of them. I read through some of the posts. People have been listing their "Top 10" memories, mostly funny incidents, the material of inside jokes.

I want to say hello. I want to reach out to them, to let them know I'm here. But I hesitate.

Twenty years.

I hover, observe, remaining unobserved, invisible. Just like back then. But it's different this time. I just want to find the right words. Because once you click "share" your words are out there forever. These people don't know me anymore, and I want to leave the right impression. It's so easy to come across as stupid in posts. I'll write a comment soon. I just need to figure out what to say.

In that quiet hour when the kids are finally in bed and the dishes washed, I open my closet, push the clothing aside, and pull out my box of YES memorabilia.

I carry the box to the dining room and spread the contents out on the table. There are old programs, pages from scripts, newspaper clippings. All in black and white, like an old movie. With each item I pick up and turn over in my hands, memories race back. Here's the program from the first summer festival, glossy pages bursting with expectation. A schedule of the shows, with dates, times and theatre numbers listed. Part of a script I'd completely forgotten about. Brittle newspaper clippings about the summer festival. An interview with the director. More scripts, in courier font, held together by staples and paperclips, my notes scribbled in the margins.

A sheet of loose leaf, handwritten in pencil: "*Scene 1: A View from the Bridge. This first scene is not only an introduction to the play, but almost a summary. The idea is that the seven people on stage are all one person. It's a battle between the rational and the irrational sides of the mind; the practical side and the idealistic.*"

It takes several moments before I realize this is a description of *Fence*, the play we performed in Europe. I stare at the sheet, and a few of the scenes slowly resurface. Until now, all I remembered was that it had to do with war and conflict, and that it was very abstract.

I dig deeper into the box. At the bottom are my two photo albums from the European tour. I lift them out. They're the old kind: the pages have a sticky background covered by a clear plastic sheet. You peel back the sheet, place your photos, then press the plastic back down, trying to smooth out the wrinkles. I turn the pages slowly. They've yellowed. In one album, the glue has dried and the photos are sliding around. I haven't looked at these albums in a long, long time. The photos are smaller than I remembered. And they're all so blurry. I thought I was a better photographer than that. Or was it the camera? Finally I realize the fuzziness comes from fading. The colours have become washed out; the contrast is gone.

Here's Lulu, posing with puckered red lips in front of the Bulldog bar in Amsterdam. Here's Sean, in that faded jean jacket I loved so much, standing at a bus stop with Brendan and Olivier making "mouth music," as I had titled it (my first encounter with beatboxing). Here's Brendan dancing with Solange on the empty stage in Brussels. Here's a group shot, taken in front of a chartered bus.

Everyone else in the photos looks so hip, so cool. I look awful. Awkward, ugly. Bulky clothing, long unshaped hair that stretches my face and somehow draws attention to my nose. Huge glasses. Ugh. And funny how I have all these pictures of other people in action, acting silly or dramatic, doing things. But that was me: always the observer, the outsider, the anti-participant.

The house is quiet. The refrigerator hums.

Looking through the clippings, the faded, photocopied pages of typewritten scripts, the photos, I start to remember. I begin to make a mental list of my own "Top 10" moments. But I'm not ready to post it on Facebook. I don't want to put it out here just yet. I wait. I hover. I hesitate. Just a few keystrokes separating thought from action, fantasy from reality.

And then I find the diary.

Montreal, October --- , 1986

Dear Diary,

We leave tomorrow. We had our final rehearsal this morning. Celia said she was proud of us and gave the usual rah-rah pep talk—not that we needed it, everyone is so excited. Europe, here we come!

I'm excited but anxious. Everyone in the play seems to have bonded but me. I suppose it's my own fault but I have no idea how to change the situation. It's almost as if it's too late. I've built this barrier and the more I think about it, the higher and stronger it gets.

My father had brought me to the airport. Everyone came with their parents, but I was still embarrassed. I didn't want to share this world with my Dad; he didn't understand. Once my bags were checked and he saw there were adults in charge, he gave me a hug. "Have a good time, cookie!"

On the plane I sat beside Olivier. His hair was the definition of tousled and blond, the kind you just want to run your fingers through. He was one of the kindest and gentlest people in the group. A good actor, too. Well, pretty much everyone on the tour was a better actor than I was. I still wasn't sure why Celia had chosen me to be part of the tour, but I was ecstatic and thankful that she had.

The flight attendants handed out dinner in those self-contained packages that were so much fun to open. There was Gouda cheese. Olivier turned to me, held up the packet and said, "Now that's a good-a-cheese!" It was a silly pun but it made me happy.

Hisako was terrified of flying and so she drank. I didn't know her well, only that she was a dancer and studying to be a professional actress. Everyone had a choice of red or white wine with their meal, but Hisako snuck into the area where the wine was kept and pocketed several bottles. I'd never seen someone so truly terrified of flying. Or so drunk. Lulu got sick on the plane too. Maybe it was alcohol or maybe just nerves. When we landed in Amsterdam, they both rushed to the bathroom and Lulu held back Hisako's long dark hair while she threw up in the toilet.

The hostel was pretty basic. All the girls were in one room and all the guys in another, including the adult chaperones. But there were twice as many girls, so that made eleven of us in one big room. It had bunk beds and a big bathroom with common showers and sinks. Everyone kept complaining about the lack of privacy, but I didn't mind. I was happy to be together in the same room as everyone else.

I loved Amsterdam, with its canals and winding streets and street-cars and bicycles. I loved the language with its double vowels. I took a boat tour and discovered a whole other life on the water. One house-boat was owned by a woman with a hundred cats.

Schools and youth groups came to see our play. I didn't have a big part. I was a member of the "crowd," kind of like the chorus in Greek theatre. After each show the whole cast would come out from the wings and sit on the front of the stage, legs dangling, and the audience would ask questions. Sean answered a lot of them. So did Hisako and Lulu. I listened, fascinated at the ease with which they expressed themselves.

A child's cry jolts me back to the present. Like a startled rabbit, I straighten and freeze, straining to hear if one of the kids has woken up. Silence. Maybe Alex is having a bad dream again. I relax but skip ahead in the diary, scanning the entries. Then, a passage clutches hold of my stomach.

... this pain in my gut, boring a hole, and it's getting deeper and deeper. I saw Olivier give Lulu a hug this morning and I wanted to cry. Every little incident reminds me that I don't belong, pushes me further into my hole. Now I'm so far down the hole that it seems impossible to climb out. I can't just come down to breakfast one morning and give everybody hugs like Lulu does, and ask brightly, "So what are we doing today?" The relationships and attitudes have been set.

I have to talk to somebody. Maybe Sean. He has such an easy time communicating with people. He always seems to know what to say.

But I have no idea how to approach him.

It was early afternoon and I was sitting on the top bunk, writing in my diary. Everyone else was out. There was a knock on the door, and then Sean poked his head in. My heart leapt.

"Is Lulu here?" he asked.

"Uh, no. I think she's downstairs."

"I didn't see her. Thought she might be up here."

"Oh. Well. I don't know."

There must be something else I could say. But I didn't know what. Sean waited a minute at the doorway.

"Well, see you later, I guess," he said finally.

"Sure."

The moment he shut the door, I started kicking myself. Story of my life.

From Amsterdam we took a bus to Brussels. Our days were a blur of rehearsals, reworking scenes, making changes.

When we weren't rehearsing or performing, I explored the city. Usually on my own. I told myself I preferred it that way. Across the crowded cobblestone square of the Grand-Place, gaping up at the Gothic and Baroque stone buildings. Past restaurants displaying their seafood wares out front on tables of ice. Past chocolate shops. Through the manicured public gardens dotted with statues and sculptures. All so unlike anything I knew back home.

One morning I wandered through the empty theatre to find Solange and Brendan dancing on stage. My heart tightened. There was such chemistry between them. I felt like I'd intruded. But when I asked if I could take a picture, they posed for the camera.

I was sitting on my bed reading when Hisako came in. The intrusion made me jump. The girls were divided into separate rooms this time, and Hisako and I hardly ever spoke to each other.

She asked me what was wrong.

"Nothing," I said.

She sat down on the bed and took the book from my hands. I watched as she turned it over to see the cover: *Life is Elsewhere*, by Milan Kundera.

"Look, you don't have to talk to me," she said. "Sometimes guys are easier to talk to. Like maybe Olivier, or Sean. They're pretty good listeners."

I looked down at the bedspread. It was a ribbed blue cotton, worn thin with use. A lump was making my throat ache.

"We're all here together," Hisako said. "Sometimes it's good to just walk up to someone and ask for a hug. Anyone here would understand that."

A hug was what I wanted more than anything.

She handed the book back to me and left the room.

The next morning, as everyone filtered into the rehearsal space, Olivier came over and said, "Hi." My insides jumped. I was surprised any time anyone started talking to me. I had no idea what to say or what to do with myself. And then he gave me a hug! Hisako must have said something to him.

The trip was almost over. Our departure date loomed like an ultimatum: I couldn't go back still feeling this way.

It was early evening, and everyone was hanging out in their rooms. Tomorrow was our final performance. Tonight we were going to a club, a last night out on the town.

I sauntered into the guys' room, as casually as I could, to join the conversation. Or to listen, anyway. I wasn't very good at joining conversations. But I'd made a decision.

Sean was standing in front of the mirror, combing his hair and fooling around with some sort of gel. I took a seat behind him, on the bed. I could see his reflection in the mirror, and my own. There were other people in the cramped room. Brendan, legs hanging over the side of the top bunk, plucking away at a guitar. Olivier, cross-legged on the floor, writing in a notebook. My insides were a thrashing sea. Twisting into a knot. I had decided that I would talk to Sean. If I could just let it out, tell someone what was going on, everything would be better. I wouldn't be alone anymore.

I sat there and watched Sean comb his hair into a peak. He laughed and then decided to try something else. There I was, just inches from him. All I had to say was, "Sean, can I talk to you for a minute?" and it would be out, the ice broken, the barrier brought down, the bottle uncorked. I said the words over and over again in my head. Just those few words, to break through from fantasy to reality. In fact, all I had to do was say his name. Then the spell would be broken. I just had to open my mouth, push the air through my vocal chords, shape the syllables with my lips and tongue. Just one word separated me from being trapped inside myself and being present in the real world. I felt like I was getting ready to jump off the highest diving board I'd ever seen. Nothing had ever seemed so difficult.

Shyness is so much more than feeling self-conscious. Years later, I'd read studies by psychologists and learn that being constantly worried about what others might think and feeling like you're unable to make an effective contribution are core characteristics of shyness. Characteristics that were no doubt further amplified by my developing teenage brain.

People would tell me, "Just be yourself." But I *was* being myself. Shyness was my default. Showing or sharing your feelings was an alien concept. Things that seemed to come naturally to other people—how to behave in certain situations, appropriate or conventional responses—were foreign to me. From my earliest years, I'd developed the defensive, safe strategy of hiding in the background. In doing so, I'd denied myself the opportunity to develop the very skills I lacked.

I know all this now.

I know now that my experience was not even unique.

But at the time, all I knew was that I felt utterly, desperately alone.

I sat there watching Sean's reflection in the mirror. I observed the strands of dark hair parting through the teeth of the comb as he brought it across his head in slow, deliberate strokes. My heart was pounding in my ears. My hands were trembling. I slid them under my thighs and sat on them.

Brendan was humming along with his guitar. He made some comment. Olivier laughed and said something in response. Sean turned his head from side to side, admiring his work.

It was clearly a boys' room. Socks, T-shirts and jeans lay in little heaps on the floor, audio-cassettes were scattered about, books and an electric shaver spilled from a knapsack. An orange peel sat on the dresser alongside a dog-eared script. The room had a musty smell, a mix of dirty socks and aftershave.

"Sean."

It was like throwing a hundred-pound medicine ball.

He looked up at my reflection.

"Can we talk?" I said.

As if he'd been expecting this, he nodded and put his comb down. He walked out into the hall and I followed. My face was hot. My legs were shaking. I didn't look at his roommates.

We sat on the floor and I took a deep breath.

"I just don't feel part of the group," I said.

Sean drew his legs up and put his arms around his knees, watching me.

I focused on a crack between the floor tiles and tried to explain what I was feeling. It wasn't easy, but it was so much easier than I thought it would be. The words came out in a jumble, not at all as I'd planned. After I finished, I kept staring at that crack. The tiles were a discoloured grey, worn from use.

Out of the corner of my eye, I saw Sean stretch his legs again, lean back onto the wall. He told me that several people had noticed that I wasn't comfortable and that I was upset. He told me they all wanted me to feel part of the group.

"You have to let go a bit, take some chances," he said. "If you talk to people, they'll listen. People want to get to know you."

He was silent for a moment, and so I looked up. He seemed to be looking at something far away. Then he told me a story about his sister, something about how she was always needy and took everyone for granted and never knew how to thank people. Then one day, she wrote him a letter. Thank you, it said. It was the most beautiful letter he'd ever received.

I wasn't exactly sure how this story was related to my situation. Was he saying I was ungrateful? Needy? My heart sank. Yet somehow, the story still helped.

Then he gave me a big hug. I clung to him. I never wanted it to end. I was also afraid that if I let go, I'd start to cry.

Lulu popped her head out of her room to tell us it was time to get ready. So that was it. We stood up and Sean went back to his room to get changed. But I felt relieved. Nothing was resolved, but I felt like a tumour had been removed from my gut.

I followed Lulu into our room to get dressed. I wasn't sure what to wear. I didn't have anything appropriate.

"Here, try this," Lulu said, digging out a khaki cotton miniskirt from her own bag. I put it on over my black tights. It fit. I'd never worn a miniskirt before.

"What should I wear on top?" I asked.

Lulu looked through my clothes and pulled out a black acrylic sweater with a wide V-neck.

"Put this on. Wait—turn it around so the V is in back. Yeah, like that. Perfect!" The wide V made the sweater droop slightly off my shoulder, like in the movie *Flashdance*. Then Lulu said, "Would you let me do your hair and make-up?"

I nodded. It felt so good to have someone take me under their wing.

Lulu had me bend my head over so that my shoulder-length hair fell completely upside down, and then emptied half a can of hairspray into it. I closed my eyes and tried not to breathe. Then Lulu brought my head up again and sprayed some more, making sure the hair kept its volume but stayed out of my face. She teased the front strands with her fingers.

After that, it was make-up time. She pushed aside my black eye-liner and took out her own plum-coloured pencil. My eyes watered as I tried to keep them open while she worked. Then, came eyeshadow and mascara.

"You have such long lashes," she said. "A lot of girls would kill for these."

Finally, bold red lipstick—Lulu's trademark. The transformation was complete. I looked in the mirror and was very pleased.

When I came out of the room, there were whistles. Sean flashed me a grin.

"Wow," he said, "you look fantastic!"

I felt my cheeks go red under the blush that Lulu had applied.

"Thanks. It's all Lulu."

"No," he said. "It's you."

At the club, I sat with some of the girls in a row of chairs near the dance floor. Music blared. People moved through the smoke-filled darkness, bodies and limbs caught in the flashes of a strobe light. I didn't drink but was feeling the buzz of being all dressed up and out on the town with the gang. I belonged. The new me.

I started nodding my head to the music. Lulu noticed and gave me a thumbs-up. I smiled but stopped moving, self-conscious.

Then, someone—I'm not even sure who—pulled me to the dance floor. At first I felt awkward, standing there with the others, trying to move my feet and hands to the beat, feeling jerky and uncoordinated. I didn't know where to look—at the faces near me or at my own hands and feet.

But then I closed my eyes. And, for a few seconds ... I let go. I stopped thinking. About myself, about everyone else. I let the music wash over me.

The beat pulsed through me, making my body sway and my feet light.

The music turned into a wispy substance and my arms and legs moved through it, buoyant, weightless.

Only the music and the dancing existed.

And then my arm made contact with other flesh. I stopped and opened my eyes. I'd bumped into another girl. She hadn't even noticed and kept on dancing. I tried to re-enter my trance, but now I felt ridiculous. After a few jerky movements I went back to my chair on the sidelines.

Still, tonight I had danced. Tonight I had dared.

The next afternoon was our last show. When it was over and the stage went to black, we all stood there for a moment, not wanting to move. Later we went for dinner. There was lots of reminiscing about the last two weeks, lots of laughing. Lulu and Hisako cried openly.

I was really going to miss everyone. I couldn't stand to think about it.

Sean came into my room while I was packing. He took my hands and said, "We've got a lot to learn from each other. This is just the first chapter." Then he wrapped his arms around me in a hug.

Dear Diary,

We're on the plane home. In five hours, I'll be back in Montreal. It's been such an incredible trip. So much has happened.

I've come to a decision: I am going to change. I have to. I've got to start showing my feelings more and telling people what I think. It's going to be hard, but I'm tired of being trapped inside myself. I'm tired of always being on the sidelines. I've got to start taking chances. A few days ago I didn't think I had the strength, but since my conversation with Sean and last night's dancing, I feel like I can do it.

I know I can.

I put down the diary. I close my eyes, digging my palms into my eye sockets.

My life now is Aviva, two and a half, soft blond curls, a warm little face that comes right up to mine and plants tiny wet kisses on my cheek. She holds my head in her two little hands, taking charge. We rub noses and she giggles. She is determined and assertive. She stands with her hands on her hips, brow furrowed, declarative. Always chattering away, the social butterfly, joining in other children's games.

My life now is Alex, shy, moody, sensitive like his parents. One minute, all little boy, running through the house with his high-speed train flying on invisible tracks in the air, jumping on the sofa, making silly faces; the next, a studious five-year-old, amazing me with his probing questions and keen leaps of logic.

My life is also my husband. Protective, caring. Quick-witted, a problem solver, a doer. But also a romantic and a dreamer. Feeling the world but not showing it.

And me? Different from twenty years ago, to be sure. Engaged with people, with life. But still, there are moments. Moments when I realize I've missed a cue. Moments when the wall goes up again.

I open my eyes, stand up and wander into the living room. The Lego has been pushed into a neat pile in the middle of the carpet, a half-built spaceship waiting for morning. I run my fingers across the spines of the books lining the shelves—novels, short story collections. Dictionaries for my translation work, thesauruses, style manuals. Of course they're all available electronically now, but sometimes I want the physical connection with paper between my fingertips. Rows of magazines. Boxes of newspaper clippings, some of them my own. A literary journal containing one of my short stories.

A truck rumbles by outside. I glance at the leaves of the birch tree, outlined by the streetlight, and open the window. Cool air rushes in.

I can't help cringing when I think back to that conversation, all those years ago, with Sean. But I am also struck by how much patience and compassion he had. How mature he was for his seventeen or eighteen years. At not quite sixteen, I must have seemed like a little sister to him.

Lulu. I wonder if she noticed that, after that night, a khaki miniskirt and black sweater became my go-to outfit. I still wear plum eyeliner.

And Celia. She believed in me. Not just by bringing me on that tour. Throughout my years at YES, she encouraged me to write, to sing, to make things happen. She wasn't just like that with me; she believed in all young people. It's why she founded the group. But that didn't make her belief in me any less strong.

It's easy to see now that I was so wrapped up in myself, and so fearful of what others might think, that I couldn't see what they were really doing for me.

The night air caresses my face. High above the empty street, the treetops stir in the breeze, leaves rustling, whispering.

After a while I close the window again.

I go back into the dining room and push the papers aside to clear a space for my laptop.

Time to say a Facebook hello.

And perhaps, also, to write some long overdue letters of thanks.

Notes on the Stories

Earlier versions of the following stories have been previously published:

- "How to Summarize Your Life in Three Metro Stops" was first published in *lichen literary journal*, Fall 2003 (vol. 5, no. 2).
- "The Understudy" was first published in *JMWW Journal* on February 26, 2020 (online).
- "Social Clues" was first published in *The Nasiona*, Issue 24, Spring 2021 (online).
- "Between the Rows" was first published in *Glint Literary Journal*, Issue 11, December 2020 (online).
- "Lost: Morris Listowel Piano" was first published in *Quebec Heritage News*, Fall 2012. A shortened version was published in the online edition of *Maisonneuve Magazine*, on August 13, 2013.
- "Tiny Fists" was first published in *Cahoots*, an online alternative women's magazine (now defunct), in August 2008.
- "Summer Evenings After Dinner" was first published in *Grain Magazine*, Volume 50.1, Fall 2022.
- "The New Door" was first published in *Quebec Heritage News*, Summer 2013.
- "The Girl in the Khaki Miniskirt" was first published as "Young Expressions" in *Shy: An Anthology*, edited by Naomi K. Lewis and Rona Altrows, University of Alberta Press, October 2013. While the names of people and of the performing arts organization have been changed, *Fence* was the real name of the play, written by Jean-Frédéric Messier.

Definitions in "Writer Emerging" are from the online Oxford English Dictionary, https://en.oxforddictionaries.com/definition/realize (accessed April 29, 2019).

Acknowledgements

I'd like to first thank the entire team at Guernica Editions for making this book possible, especially Michael Mirolla, for taking a chance on me, and Kulamrit Bamrah, for his editing expertise and patience.

Over the years, so many different people have played a significant role at different stages of my writing journey leading up to the publication of this book. Their support and encouragement have been invaluable. In particular, I'd like to extend my heartfelt gratitude:

To Claire Holden Rothman, for her generous guidance and mentorship, her steadfast support and encouragement, and for convincing me that I could publish a book. Also for suggesting the title "Voice Lessons."

To Nicole Breit, for introducing me to alternative short literary forms, as well as a supportive online community of like-minded writers, and for her warm friendship.

To Rachel Laverdiere, for her vital feedback on the first complete draft of the manuscript, for her perceptive critiques of later stories, for being my "accountability buddy," and for her infectious energy and optimism.

To Rachel Thompson, for renewing my self-confidence by helping me get published again in a literary journal after seven years of rejections, and for including me in a warm, supportive online writing community.

To Joel Yanofsky, for his guidance during the StoryNet Non-Fiction Mentorship Program offered by the Quebec Writers' Federation, and his generous advice years later when I started sending out this manuscript. I only wish you were here to see the result.

To Elaine Kalman Naves, for her comment at a party many years ago which, unbeknownst to her, started me on the path to this book: she reassured me that if I was feeling uninspired, it was okay to go back and revisit stories that I'd written in the past. ("No, it's not cheating," she said.)

To Heather Diamond and Lucy Wilkinson, for their ongoing support and encouragement in all things writing and submitting. To Susan Olding, for sharing her wisdom and experience.

To Trish, Aura and Shadi for the inspiration gained during our writing group, short-lived as it was.

To Malcolm Thomas, my first long-distance writing exchange partner, pre-email, for his constructive feedback and encouragement.

To Stéphane and Gabriel, for reading my early stories and believing in me.

To Julie, for being a reliable sounding board and sharing my hopes and insecurities.

To Lena, for being a trusted friend.

To the many teachers, writers and participants in workshops over the years who read and commented on my stories.

To the people in my stories, whether they wanted to be in them or not, but especially Christine H., Clare S., Marc N. and Laurie K.: please consider this book as the thank-you letter I never wrote.

To Jonathan, Max and Samantha, for their unconditional love and devotion.

Thank you all for believing in me. You have helped get my voice out into the world.

About the Author

Eve Krakow is a writer, translator, singer and mom. Her stories have appeared in various literary magazines and an anthology. Through her writing, she seeks to reach others by giving form to that quiet yet insistent inner voice that longs for human connection and belonging. She lives in Montreal. You can discover more about her work at evekrakow.com.

MIX
Paper
FSC® C100212
FSC
www.fsc.org

Printed by Imprimerie Gauvin
Gatineau, Québec